Ill-Mannered
Ghosts

by Nicole Sarrocco

Karate Bride

THE OCCASIONALLY TRUE NOVELS
Lit by Lightning
Ill-Mannered Ghosts

for Sydney –
happy reading!
Lit Fest Wake Forest 2018

Ill-Mannered Ghosts

An Occasionally True Account
of Hillbilly Stonehenge, Occult
Cleaning Products, the Lady in
the Picture, and the Bloodcurdling
Tale of Crybaby Lane

by Nicole Sarrocco

CHATWIN BOOKS
SEATTLE 2016

Cover design by Annie Brulé. Photograph of the author by
Jason Hedrick. Edited by Phil Bevis.

This is a work of fiction. No resemblance is intended to any
living person, except for kin. Unless you think you recognize
yourself—then it's *really* all about you.

paperback ISBN 978-1-63398-035-8

hardcover ISBN 978-1-63398-040-2
(special hardcover limited edition)

Chatwin Books
www.chatwinbooks.com

to Jason

CONTENTS

A short and true story that begins *"One time, in Myrtle Beach…"*

I knew these particular gypsies, because one of them, Ziggy, played accordion in my dad's restaurant and lived in Myrtle during the off season. We'd all come down to the beach for the weekend: me, the waiters, the accordion-playing gypsy, and we'd been drinking all day, gin and fruit juice out of plastic bottles. We ended up back at the gypsy trailer park. We met Tzigane there, Ziggy's girl, and she tried to read everybody's cards but the boys weren't interested. Tzigane pulled a book off the shelf to show me — André Gide — and while I was talking, she dealt.

She made four rows, and then she asked me questions. After my answer, she'd watch me for a second, then whisper numbers to herself until she picked up one of the cards. Three times she picked up the Jack of Spades. Ziggy had come to the doorway, holding a Budweiser in his massive hand. She looked up at him and straightened her lips.

Ziggy laughed. "All it means," he said, holding his free hand toward me with the palm up, "is that he's in your past, this dark man. He's in your present, too, but you know it. That's good. It means you can keep an eye on him."

Tzigane folded her arms and leaned back, still watching Ziggy.

"Well, I know," he nodded and paused for a long sip of beer. "But she's lucky by nature. And the future can always be changed."

CHAPTER ONE

IT'S A TERRIBLE TASTE—bitter, earthy, dirty. But it's something I recognize from childhood and can't place. I woke up choking on it, the unfamiliar shape in my mouth in the dark room, disoriented. A dream? I hope it's a dream, a terrible one, and I've had a lot of those lately.

Man, do I ever hate throwing up. Thomas makes fun of me when I'm hung over, curled in a ball, fighting the inevitable. But this time I stuck my fingers down my throat in the sinking darkness, put my sweaty forehead down on the cold kitchen counter. I have some really nice kitchen counters. They make me feel grown up. When I used to come home from college, I used to put my head down on my mother's kitchen counters because they were so big and clean and cool. Made out of some kind of pricey stuff, like granite. Corian? Is that a thing? It sounds like a Shakespeare villain.

I have to stop making up so much utter crap in my head. It's ruining my ability to focus on real things. For instance, what did I just almost swallow? This is no way to wake up from a disco nap on date night.

There it is. Oblong and mottled beige, hanging out there in the sink, a little worse for wear. Wait. I know what that is. That's the dog's heartworm pill. So I'm guessing I rolled up my antihistamine in a piece of deli ham and it is now inside the dog.

"Sorry, Toast. I'm gonna need that back."

No use, though. Dogs don't choke on strange things. It's a major tenet of dog philosophy. Whatever it is, go ahead and eat it. You can always throw it up later.

To top it off, I think I just rested my head in a puddle of ghostly ectoplasm on the kitchen counter. There's sticky stuff all over my cheek. Lately I can't seem to wipe everything down often enough to keep that creepy residue under control. God, does nobody in this family know how to operate a bottle of Fantastic and a handful of paper towels? Clean a kitchen counter, people. Okay, that there's Koolaid, but this over here—this is ectoplasm.

As I'm sticking my finger down my dog's throat, all I can think about is Groucho Marx saying "Inside of a dog, it's too dark to read." I think she swallowed it already. Of course she swallowed it already. Maybe I should go ahead and Google it now. "Dog. Antihistamine. Accidental ingestion."

I have a four year old, so I can't prove that stuff is ectoplasm. I also can't prove it's ectoplasm because there's no lab test or anything. I Googled that, too, a while ago when the goo started showing up on the countertop every day at about four o'clock.

Internet, I refuse to believe that this is the first time a tired woman accidentally fed her dog an antihistamine. I go ahead and Google "Human. Canine Heartworm medication. Accidental ingestion." Try that little search out for yourself sometime; it's instructive.

"Accidental." I don't know why it's so important to me that I make it clear to the Internet that I didn't intentionally feed my dog my antihistamines. But maybe I'm just paranoid that an hour after I type it in, the SPCA will send black helicopters. I heard they do that. This question is truly not the worst one someone will ask Google today. It's not the worst question it's being asked right this minute.

"Chemicals that will dissolve a human skeleton."
"Forensically undetectable poisons."
"How to disable brakes on a Toyota."
"Where can I get a used pregnancy test with a positive result?"
"How to remove Sharpie marker from baby skin."
"Needed: a three–to-four year old Siamese cat. Must replace damaged exactly."

All around the world, people are doing bad things to one another. Right this second.

Yeah, the last year got away from us a few times, and once or twice it got kind of bad for me. But we all learned a lot. That's one way we handle the bad stuff. We talk about how educational it is. It can be, at least. Not always. And not always proportionally educational, but you move on, and new knowledge is a kind of handrail in the dark. While the lightning is striking, you can at least get a good look around. A flash of something useful. There are always people who should be here still who are not anymore. And then there are people who ought to have been gone a long time ago who are still inexplicably here.

If you'd been around last year when Thomas and I managed to install Granny's ashes under the new library, you'd know why all the electronics in the house have been behaving better since then. No more suspicious hairbrush relocations, either. The vacuum turned up again, in good news, but the iron is still missing. I'd buy another one, but it feels like giving up. I know it's in this house someplace. I'm no more enthusiastic about housekeeping than she was, so I always interpreted the interference with appliances as a benevolent, if inconvenient, sort of intervention. But nothing new has disappeared in a while, so there has been a shift, and probably, possibly, for the better. I'm rumpled but happier.

Ectoplasm from nowhere, objects popping in and out. Bad dreams. Inappropriate Internet searches. That's my new normal. I'm improvising. Lacking any chapter in any known etiquette book or page on Pinterest to handle such things.

Only after it stopped did I realize how particular Granny's behavior had been. The appliances, the car not starting—her live-and-let-live relationship with dust and clutter, her agoraphobia. But the hairbrush. I kept thinking about her perfect pin curls and her Chanel No. 5, and hiding the hairbrush seemed like a judgment or something, until I remembered how when I was a little girl I'd hide from my mom when she'd try to brush my hair. I'd cry the whole time—to be fair, my mom didn't know how sensitive my scalp actually was and thought I was just being a jerk. My mom could hang by her hair from a hook like a circus freak and she'd be fine, but I can hardly get mine into a ponytail without feeling that one agonizing hair that's pulling the wrong way, and if I leave it up for too long, I get a headache. But it's crazy curly hair, it grows out instead of down once it gets to my shoulders, and the disarray bothered my mother. More importantly it bothered my father. He'd come home after a week on the road and the first thing he'd say would be, "Kid's hair is a rat's nest. Has she been living in the crawl space all week? Shit. She looks like the lost member of the Manson family."

But the more my mother would tear and tear at my hair, the angrier my hair would get, a cloud of wires without a trace of the curl, kinetic sculpture, a colony of sleepy hedgehogs. I'd hide at my grandmother's house, under her bed. In the armoire. The one with the whispery voices. The bad armoire. And my mother usually gave up before she'd ever find me in there behind my grandmother's leopard and muskrat coats, my ear to the dark wood, my eyes closed in case any of the voices ever showed a mouth or a face.

Google's answers are rarely consoling. I don't know why I even bother to ask. I'm still standing next to the stove, trying to read these results on my phone without my glasses because I was only halfway ready to go out to dinner when I came in here after my disco nap to give the dog her pill, two days overdue, because I keep forgetting. Thomas will be back from dropping off the kids at my mom's any minute now. Still no shoes, still can't decide if this sweater is okay to wear with the hole in the sleeve. And my hair is a disaster. Do you people have to call it "date night"? So much pressure to get everything right.

I rest my cheek on my hand. And find a handful of cold, lumpy ectoplasm.

CHAPTER TWO

WE ALWAYS PLAN TO GO to a fancy new place, because there's so many now. You can't hardly get mac and cheese in downtown Raleigh without lobster in it, and you can't swing a dead cat in Durham without hitting a plateful of charcuterie. But as usual, we're at the lesbian bar.

"I've got something I want to try out on you."

Well, I knew it wasn't a new menu item. We always get their roast beef sandwiches, French Dips called I Put My Hand Upon Your Hip. The fun starts as soon as you order. And big glasses of bourbon, because that's how they come here.

"I know lately you've been looking for ways to make your transmissions more useful, so I was reading an article online the other day—"

"Are we going to talk about permittivity again? I didn't bring my notes, and I want to keep up. I think we're onto something."

"No, no—totally new approach."

Thomas's engineering approach to fine-tuning my ghost story antenna has been turning out to be a pretty effective one, and overall grounding in its effect. Grounding, ha ha. See what I did there? But really, once all my history started spilling out, he set about putting sense to it. Which is a good thing, because there's not a chance of backing out with a flip comment like, "Oh hey, my bad! I just watched too much 'Touched by a Ghost Whisperer' and my head was pudding. Once I turned the TV off, the voices stopped talking to me."

That's not how it works anyway, as I've explained.

These days, Thomas looks for the parameters of this thing I've got, my spooky podcasts. Even if I only showed it all to him by accident and sideways at first. I think he knows what worries me most is my propensity to be hijacked by the narratives of the dead. At first it was scary. This was the very set of questions I'd been avoiding since childhood, shouting into rooms how I didn't want to hear anything about what went on in there, and by God I had better not see anything of what went on in there. Now I'm a little scared of failing some kind of test. I'll never really believe this isn't a kind of crazy. You're running a little test in your head right now, listening to me explaining all of this. That's okay. I know that look. Everybody does it.

"First of all, this is not a test, so don't even think of it that way. Well, it's a test, but this hasn't really been your thing before. I just found this website and... I'll explain how it works in a minute. But I just want to see what you get out of this. Trust me?"

Trust you? With my life, and more than once, so yeah, let's see what you've got. If didn't trust you, how would I have ever gotten Granny's ashes interred under that new library in Forsythe County? And I didn't even get struck by lightning doing it. And once I figure out what to do with that other set of ashes, I know who will be there to help me.

"First let me ask if there's any chance that a strong performance might have a financial or social benefit of some kind?"

"Not a bit. Just interesting." Thomas doesn't lie. He's having fun, though, and his curiosity and patience have made these last few months a lot more bearable. Almost fun.

"What the hell. Let's give it a shot."

Thomas fiddled with his phone for a minute, then he set the thing in front of me, but kept the screen covered with his hand.

"Don't look at it yet. Okay. Clear your mind, and when you look at the picture, just think to yourself, Do I trust this person?"

There was a photograph of a young boy on it. A heartbreaking young boy of about twelve or thirteen. He reminded me of one of my students, except the picture was really old.

"Just yes or no. Do you trust him."

"Oh yes," I said, because that question seemed terribly beside the point for this pained boy who was thinking very hard about his mother. Then, I felt dizzy. Downward. Knees buckling as something hit me hard in the torso. I was glad I was sitting.

"What is it?"

"I'm falling down."

"Do you recognize him?"

"Yes. No. I'm not sure. Maybe. Would I know who he is?"

"You might. I thought about leaving this one out, but I decided to start with it anyway."

"Well jeez. Who is it? He's so sad. Something about his mother—either he misses her, or he's just so... his love for his mother is breathtaking. I can't get past that."

"And you felt like you were falling?"

"Yes, but just a short—like to my knees. To the ground. I can't... it's unfamiliar. But kind of like the wind knocked out of me. Okay, who is it? I feel like I can't breathe, but I think he's just stressing me out with those eyes. Tell me. He's really sad."

"He's a poet named Federico..."

"Oh, LORCA. It's Lorca."

"Did you recognize him?"

"Well, now I'm not sure. I certainly know who it is. I've seen pictures of him older, definitely. I can see it now. I must have registered it somehow."

"Yeah, well, you know how he died, then."

For a minute, all I could remember was Hart Crane and the boat, but then I remembered Lorca.

"Because your description was kind of... accurate."

"Well, so maybe I recognized Lorca. I'm going to fold on this one—I'm not sure this proves much."

"Wait, though... there's more. Keep your fork."

So we ordered two more bourbons, one with Coke, one without.

The next picture was more recent. Thomas asked me the same question.

"All right. Same thing: just yes or no. Do you trust this guy?"

"No." Definitely not. No way.

"You answered pretty fast. You sure?"

"Now don't editorialize."

"I'm not. I thought about that, actually, and I know how big your antenna is, so I'm really trying not to send any... vibes or whatever. There's this whole series of questions on the site, and I'm just going through them. We didn't do it before because you knew the guy. And it says to take your time, so I'm just checking."

"No. 'No' is my final answer."

"Okay. Next question. What is important to this person?"

I stopped for a second, not looking at Thomas because I didn't want to read his expression. He's got a decent poker face, better than most people, whose faces are all like newspapers. But I didn't want to get anything. I was getting invested in this experiment.

"Don't you want to know why I don't trust him?"

"You go ahead and talk about whatever you want. I'm just reading the questions. Say whatever comes into your head."

"Is that what the rules say?"

"There aren't really any rules. There's just these photos and the questions..."

"But you know who this is."

"Yes. I've got the key. Bios of all the people in the pictures."

"Did you read it already?" I still didn't look at Thomas. I was studying the mouth of the man in the photograph, his lips stretched in a muted snarl. He looked startled.

"Just this one. I'm only reading one at a time. Yeah, I know who he is."

"But he's not famous? This one?"

"No. He's not a famous person. You should say what you're thinking instead of asking me a bunch of questions. You'll end up saying you just read me."

Thomas smiled and put his hand over my hands on the bar for a minute, like a turtle shell. I felt knotted up looking at the photo. This one was scared, too, but he was no good.

"He's sorry for all the shame. Sorry to his mother. No—older. Grandmother."

I felt Thomas shift just a little, but I still didn't look at him. I stared at the man.

"He keeps moving a little. Something's changing. He's not who he says he is. It's like he's an amnesia victim or something. I keep wanting to say it's not about the money."

Thomas snorted suddenly, muffled, into his drink, so I stopped.

"I'm really sorry. But that was effing weird. I'll go with you had some subconscious knowledge on the last one, but there's just no way on this—you've never seen this website or these pictures?"

"I don't have a clue about any of this. I wouldn't even have known how to find such a thing. How do you Google 'random people I wouldn't know but who have discernable issues?'"

"Okay. You may as well know on this one. He's Norway's most infamous grifter, a thief who, using multiple identities, robbed a series of people of their life savings over a twelve year period…"

"Wow. Yeah, I knew he was a tool. I can recognize a lying sack of shit at twenty paces."

"In court, he declared his sorrow at having disappointed his grandmother, the woman who raised him and the only human being who ever showed him true kindness."

"Hm. Maybe." More than anything, I didn't want to believe this snake really felt remorse. His crappy, belated chagrin seemed like one more con. Except I already knew it was his one moment of honesty in layer upon layer of lies. Bewildered, he'd given up any real chance at an identity years before, in childhood. Betrayed. By somebody. Something killed the real person who once lived in that body. The only thing left was the thin string of emotion that attached to his grandmother. What broke him? That part I couldn't find. I could guess, but all those thoughts were mine, based on my experience. The photo had told me all it would.

I looked at Thomas. He picked up the phone and looked at me.

"Want to try another?"

"Yeah, I do," I said, "but this time, how about you don't read the bio? I don't want to be getting this from you, and I can't tell for sure."

"Fair enough. Let's just pull up the next one, then. Okay. Oh. Okay. Here you go."

Thomas placed the phone on the bar again and stood up.

"Going to walk outside. I'll be back."

Something bothered him, so he went outside to smoke so that he wouldn't sway me with his own reaction. So before I looked, I figured, this must be some photo. I turned back around to the bar to at his phone, and there she was.

This one was the oldest photo so far, probably turn of the century, and my first inclination was that I was looking at that special Lizzie-Borden axe-wielding batshit kind of crazy. Her hair up in a deranged bun, her eyes startled but vacant, her whole physical person resembling a boarded-up haunted house. Her dress was Victorian, but old and ragged. It struck me that the photo was taken in a mental institution or something. She was not free. Not just mentally—that part was certain. But she was imprisoned in this photo. In that moment, in that room. Now, in the frame, the cell of this picture, the edges of this cell phone. Oh no. Oh no.

I looked over at Thomas's empty bar stool. The bartender had disappeared into the kitchen. There's a party to my right pre-gaming for Legends, the one decent drag bar in Raleigh, and in that minute I just wanted to go drink Red Bull and vodka with them and head around the corner at eleven to dance to Metric and forget everything I could see on this woman. Tears hit my cheeks before I felt the sting in my eyes.

She wasn't violent. That was a mistake. But an easy one to make, because everything about her shouted chaos. By the time of this photo, she'd been broken. Not defeated, though. There was something incredibly persistent in her. Hard to say whether she wouldn't let go of it, or whether it wouldn't let go of her. I felt like a courtroom, once. Maybe more than once. I felt like a gruesome parade. A public display. But she's not ashamed. She wants everyone to see her. When everyone can see her, she has hope. But it doesn't work, and she doesn't know why she's here. She knows something, but this place is wrong.

Thomas walked back in from the patio. He smiled as he crossed though the bar, and I realized then that it doesn't matter. *I can relax. This pain is not mine. This fear. This loss. None of these are mine. It's Friday night, we have a babysitter. I'm at the bar where they pour doubles for my single order, and where the drag queens talk to me about my shoes. I'm home. No one is lying to me.*

I've got a ton of crazy women in my family. I look back at her, because I want to either distance myself or comfort her, and I don't really know which it is. It's hard for me not to sympathize. As I turn my head to see her, I see white fire around the side of her head, like an ermine hat that's askew. Like a lightning halo falling off. Then it's gone. I pick up the phone and I'm staring at this photo on the screen when Thomas touches my arm and the shock makes us both laugh.

"Static. Guess I need to ground somewhere." Thomas tapped the metal edges of the bar stool.

"Look at her," I blurted out.

"Oh, I saw her," Thomas settled back into the seat and swirled the ice in his drink. "She's something else."

"No, *look* at her—do you see that light around her head?"

Thomas took the phone and held it close, then far away, squinting a little.

"I'm not sure I see what you mean. Like a shadow?"

"No! Like sharp white light, all on that side, down past her ear over there. And three flashes, here, here, and here on top." I pointed at the spots in the picture where the light had been brightest, like little explosions around her skull.

Thomas leaned forward, holding the phone in both hands. Glasses on. Glasses off. He put the phone down and sat back.

"I don't see that. But it's interesting. Do you want to do a couple of the questions? Then we'll find out who she is together."

"She's a historical figure I think. But I don't know why I think that. And I don't understand the light, but she's afraid of it. Electricity. She's afraid of the light."

"So do you trust her?"

"I do. She's not lying."

The tears started again, a little.

"Huh. That's... not what I expected at first. But I can tell already that you're not going to say what I thought."

"Oh, she's crazy," I said. "If she wasn't to start with, she is in this picture. But she can't lie. She doesn't know how. Everything fell apart and she doesn't understand. But she never lied about anything."

Thomas looked at her again. By then, I was feeling like she was sitting with us here at the bar, between us and the drag queens. *I want to hug her,* I thought. I wanted them to hug her. I wanted them to tell her she's beautiful and that being broken is beautiful, that what's left of you when the bastards have cracked you open is the most beautiful thing in the world, the truth, the platinum-blonde, cold-hard, blue-lipped song of truth, swimming in the ice lake... riding in a sleigh under the stars. Under fur. The song that the universe pulls out of you. She knows that song. The ice

made her sing it. White ice. Shards. They stuck the shards
on her head like a crown. Because she is a princess.

"She thinks they'll see her."

"Who?"

I was still crying a little, but I laughed. She is not me.

"Who will see her?"

"Somebody. Somebody will see her and they'll know."

She is not me. This pain is not mine. I do that square-
breathing thing that my yoga teacher taught me to do when
I think I might hyperventilate. It helps.

Thomas stared at the screen. His face was lit with that
blue-white glow from reading it so closely.

"Whoa, shit. Well, okay. They got me, but they didn't
fool you." He smiled over at me, then ran his hand
through his hair, touching his temple on the right side.
His eyebrows wrinkled up.

"So tell me again where you saw those lights? The
explosions?"

I pointed to where it would be on Thomas's head. Side,
top, then the spot where his fingers already rested on his
temple. "Here, here, and here."

Thomas took my hand.

"This woman was a resident at the Pennsylvania State
Sanatorium. She underwent several rounds of electroshock
therapy. I want you to see this diagram. In 1937, here's
where the electrodes would have been attached."

Thomas put the phone down. Here. Here. Here. Little
explosions.

"No one knows who she really was. But she insisted, for the last forty years of her life for which there is a record, that she was Anastasia, the lost Romanov princess."

Someone will see me, she believed, each time she was presented to the panel. *Somebody out there will recognize me. Somebody will know who I am.*

CHAPTER THREE

EARLY LAST THURSDAY MORNING, I got a phone call from
my cousin in Australia with what would have been unexpected news, had I not had a downright shocking run-in
with my estranged father a few weeks before, when he
called Mom at the office and tried to run the Nigerian
Businessman scheme on her. The shocking part was that
she listened to this horseshit to its inevitably bizarre and
insulting conclusion. To say my mother sees the good in
everyone oversimplifies her gift: she actually can't see the
bad at all. She's bullshit-blind. She can't see it piling up
when people are talking. She just dances along to the beat
of their shitsongs. She thinks there's a pony under all of it
someplace.

Anyway, as she was explaining his immodest proposal,
the core facts did slink out.

"He says if I can loan him fifty grand, he can pay off the
bank, and he'll give me ten grand now, and then we'll..."

"So the bank finally foreclosed, and he can't talk his way
out this time."

"He says they haven't actually foreclosed yet. He's still
living there, and he can stay if he gets the fifty grand by
Wednesday..."

"... he's getting in and out through the broken sliding
glass door and keeping his stuff in storage pods in the yard.
Also, he's already asked everyone else who is still actually
talking to him."

"I'm just thinking about it. I didn't say yes."

"Good, because it's no. I'm restraining myself right

now from picking up the phone and calling him, so that the first words I'll have said to him in twenty years—and the last words he'll ever hear from me—would be 'I can NOT believe you tried to run the Nigerian Businessman scheme on my mother, you jackal.'"

"Now, there's no need to do that. Don't get upset; I was just talking to him."

"That's how everything bad starts in this world."

"He's not gonna mess with me. He knows better than to do that."

"Guess that's why he called you to run the Nigerian Businessman gambit by you for twenty minutes."

"Listen, I knew that whole time what I was doing. He's not getting anything from me. Besides, he's old and sad now."

"Don't you dare feel sorry for him, now. That's how he gets you. Fuck him. He put himself right where he is. All the money you gave him is gone, he over-mortgaged his house—"

"I don't know what in the world kind of story he gave that bank to get them to lend him more money."

"That's their problem. It's about time for those banks to lose one right alongside him. Don't get in the way of this karma blizzard or it'll take you out, too."

Mom moves the papers around on her desk, looking for something. Maybe her secret cigarettes. She puts a hand on one hip and looks over at me.

"I don't feel sorry for him," she says, softly, and even though she's sad, I believe her, because I know she's not sad for him. She'd sad for us, for the years we spent living out there with a demonic presence. If he'd had guts and an organizing principle, he'd have been a serial killer. All he ended up being was a thief and a bully, a giant squalling baby who saw everybody in the world as a candy dispenser to kick until a Snickers bar fell out.

So when my cousin called me I was prepared. Sort of. Just out of bed, getting into my gym clothes, I heard the phone ringing. After my mid twenties, I assume a phone call before seven in the morning or after ten at night means somebody's in a ditch. But Charlotte wasn't in a ditch; she was in Australia.

I didn't recognize the number, but it was long. Fully expecting some kind of bank fraud call from Malaysia, because that was the week I was having, I answered.

"Charlotte! Hey! Everybody okay?" Gotta check out the ditch possibility and get that out of the way first.

"Yeah, yeah—well, everybody except Nick, but then again, I think your dad might have finally pissed everybody off enough that they don't much care. But that's only part of why I called. I guess you know he's out of the house. He was still getting in, last I heard, staying there part of the time. But the power's off and the water's off, and I think the Sheriff went out there last week... Look, you don't even need to worry about all that."

"He's not staying with Caroline?" Caroline was Charlotte's sister. She lived in the house that belonged to their mother, just across the road and around the curve from the house where I grew up.

"No, he wore out that welcome pretty fast," Charlotte sighed, halfway round the world. I pictured those old map cartouches, the goddess of wind whose breath sent the ships across the ocean. "I'd say that's over. She's fed up."

"She's a brave woman, anyway. What can I help you with? You know he called and tried to run the Nigerian Businessman scheme on Mom..."

"No he did not! You know not. Honey, I'm sorry. I guess I'm not surprised."

"He had some convoluted story about how he put the land in your husband's name—"

"That's actually why I'm—my husband's name? Are you serious? What an ass. First of all, I bought the land. I mean, Dan and I did buy it together, but—I swear, your father, even when he's not involved, he snakes his way in. We bought the land on the open market, years ago, another time the bank was about to take the house and he needed cash. He put up the land and all I could think was, if he ends up selling that land and somebody puts a trailer park out there, it's gonna be a mess. Donna, Caroline, Beth— they were all calling me. Nicole, I need to be able to come home at Christmas. I never really intended to end up stuck in this position."

I wasn't entirely sure we could afford to buy all thirty acres Charlotte and Dan had saved from becoming the trailer park nobody on the old Camden Road wanted to confront. That three mile stretch was the longest piece of road between Garner and Clayton without an aluminum house on wheels someplace. I'm not even sure how we managed to avoid it, but it was true. Some of the Camdens were still out there, nestled in neocolonial brick palaces set away from the road behind long circular driveways. And we, descendants of the Youngs and the Pipkins. We

brought no trailers. My aunt Lucinda maintained the
fragile old shipwreck of my great-grandparents house,
which had been built on the remnants of a house built
at least a century before them. That chimney still stood,
providing a firm antebellum spine to the younger house.
And the cookhouse stood behind, the repetitive motions of
rolling dough, and the sweep and crack of broken chicken
necks through the yard.

That land was full of graves. I wasn't sure about this
plan, but I grew up on that land, and I was sure what was in
it. I told Charlotte I'd have to know more.

I was really proud of myself that two or three times when
I almost called her "Charlie," I stopped myself. She doesn't
like being called "Charlie" anymore. That was a long time
ago.

CHAPTER FOUR

EDGAR CONVINCED ME. Edgar, bounding fearlessly
through the trees, short four-year-old fingers wrapping
around bits of granite he drew out of the fallow fields. It
was almost enough to make me forget a lot of things, the
way he loved it out here. Nora was photographing everything. I made a mental note to study all those pictures
later.

"What was just here?" I asked Josie, my cousin, who
lived in another adjacent house that had belonged to our
great-aunt.

"Corn! They just plowed the last of it under. Mama lets
Grady Phillips plant what he wants, and he keeps it rotated
and healthy. He lives over there off Rock Quarry, does
landscaping."

It had been twenty years since I saw any of this, except
quickly through a car window, the three or four times I'd
driven Thomas or Nora out here to see the house I grew up
in.

I had forgotten how far the fields rolled back. Growing
up, they had been full of tobacco. One year they planted
soybeans—some kind of government initiative. Years later
when I tried soymilk for the first time, I remembered the
controversy in our family and those squat plants, paler and
duller than the glossy tobacco we were used to seeing.

Aunt Lucinda wasn't home right then, so we couldn't go
inside the big house. But we walked around the big magno-
lias outside, Nora taking pictures of everything, Edgar
carrying the cat he'd found. And then when my cousin
Beth drove by, rolled down her car window and waved—her

"hey, y'all!" rolled across the lawn and the pots of geraniums and mums, the birdbath and the broken folding chair, the hammock and the buckets, up to Thomas's ear, and a broad smile broke across his face.

"I could live here," he said, exhaling deeply. I hadn't seen him light a cigarette since we'd been out here.

"Nicky, you wrote about seeing the crooked man on the stairs—you want to go see his grave? Do you remember where it is? I'll show you." Josie's rubber boots had ladybugs on them, so it was hard to be too afraid. Nora's eyes were big, and Edgar was already ahead of us, turning his head back to smile at Josie.

A bunch of the kids had all seen the Crooked Man, not just me. That made me feel better. Josie and Aunt Lucinda and Donna all said they saw him, but every time they'd talk about it Caroline would hold up one hand and say, "I did not see him," as if she wanted to abstain officially, on the record and all. "But," she'd add, "I knew he was there."

That's how things were with me. But I did see him that one time. And there was the grave, just past the plowed middle pasture, where the brambles got thick, next to a massive oak.

"That tree's at least 150 years old." Thomas stared up at it.

"The lady's out here." Edgar pointed down further into the woods. Nora was kneeling, photographing the headstone. She looked up at her brother, then slowly raised the camera and took his picture. He kept looking down into the woods.

"The lady. She's here. She has a chain."

It would have been so easy—and understandable—for my husband—any husband—to give me one of those *it's your fault our boy sees ghosts* looks... Or for that matter, for me to get one on my own account. But like always, he just rolled with it. The open-minded engineer: seeking data, working toward solutions.

"Oh well. Okay then, buddy." Thomas squeezed my arm and whispered, "Yep. That's not weird at all." He did a pretty good job of rolling with the peculiar statements that Edgar offered up from time to time. He understood. It'd be a lot better for Edgar, not having to keep it in. But standing in these woods next to a hundred-year-old grave, Edgar's description of the lady with the chain who was in the woods struck even me as a little creepy.

"She got a blue dress on."

"Oh, good," I said. "Does she need our help?"

"Nope."

It was always good to ask, I thought. Even though Edgar's responses to offers of assistance to his characters always ended in a polite but resolute negative.

"Okay, sweetie. Tell her we're okay."

"Uh huh." Edgar turned his attention to the headstone. He just glanced back at me and half-smiled.

That night, the night after the first visit, I fell asleep early, exhausted from all the hiking and talking and thinking. I woke up in the middle of the night, about three a.m., and you know how sometimes in a dream you're in a place you know doesn't exist anymore, but it really seems like you're there? I knew immediately that I was in my parents' old bedroom. Thomas was beside me, sleeping deep, even though there was a loud party going on outside by the pool. I was thinking how I should go check on Granny; it sounded like the biggest party noise was coming from right outside her apartment, and I thought she must be frightened. But I couldn't move. When I tried to pull the covers off, my hands wouldn't lift. My legs were so light they seemed not to be there. Floated away.

I heard footsteps and a scuffle sound down the dark hallway. So dark, even with all the lights on the other side, in the backyard. All the voices. Then running, little feet, and Edgar came running into the bedroom. Both of his hands were clamped tightly over his mouth, and his eyes were wide, wondrous, a little frightened. But mostly stark and round. He let go of his mouth with one hand and grabbed the side of the bed, heaving himself up next to me without meeting my eyes. He swung his free hand back over his mouth and pointed back at the dark doorway. My heart hurt against my bones. I turned slowly. There were three of them, in long capes with hoods. Where their faces should have been, only blackness.

I sat up in bed, breathing noisily and swearing. Thomas's back looked exactly as it had five minutes ago, his tattoo pin up girl still reading the same page of that book she never seemed to finish. I looked around our bedroom, thinking about how the orientation of the bed, the back door to the porch, the hallway, the bathroom—all of it was so spatially similar to my parents' old room. I hadn't noticed before. Was this a problem? Was this *whole thing* a problem? What was this dream about?

I watched Thomas as I told him all about the nightmare, waiting to see if he thought it was significant. "That sounds terrifying. Yikes." He didn't seem to be concerned, except that it had upset me. Even though I knew that the universe didn't work that way, it did have me rattled. But a good psychiatrist—heck, a crummy psychiatrist—could tell me exactly why I'd be worried about my kids out there. This land's haunted as Hell, but nothing's coming to get us.

CHAPTER FIVE

VISITING THE HOUSE I grew up in had to happen next. No way to know without going in. We didn't have a key, but growing up, keys hadn't really been necessary.

"Damn it. I've only been here for twenty minutes and I'm angry."

Thomas gave me a look. He is the only one who understands that I actually undersell things, most times. It's often more severe than my original report. The truth is, I'm precise in ways that unnerve people. You won't believe me when I say this, but I see truths the way flies see color. It's not a straight line, you know. It's like bubbles stuck on top of other bubbles.

"Sorry, baby. I know. You're coming from the garage—the garage is not a good place. Between the garage and this door to my parents' bedroom has always been a problem."

Thomas half-scratched, half-tapped his head for a second. "It's probably more that your father left his shit-tastic car in the driveway. I'm looking for him around every corner."

"Oh, that thing's been here a while. It's got no tags on it. Probably doesn't run, even." Josie came over to the house with us, and we were both rattling doors and windows looking for an easy way in. The bank had the thing locked down more than it had ever been in its life.

If there is any chance of me living on this land again, we have to see how I feel about it. And for me to know that, I need to see how Thomas reacts to it. He knows I'm checking in with him. If he didn't notice anything, I think

I'd be worried. But he definitely notices. Most people notice. Even without my father here.

Thomas has never met my father. He'd always tell people, "All I know about Nicole's father is that she showed me this picture of him and said, 'If you ever see this guy near my kids, get rid of him however you need to.' So I know my job, and he's not coming around here. That's a fact."

I was standing next to some ugly, pointy bushes where Granny's Gabriel's Trumpets used to be. There was a bunch of wooden decking now, but right here was where the biggest one had been.

"This is where Dad saw the witch."

"Okay." Thomas stared at the spiny bush like it had maybe been a witness and might still have some information.

"He said she smelled really bad, like bad breath. She laughed at him."

"I like her." Thomas said. He looked up to the top of the house. "I know that is supposed to be a new roof, but the flashing is all wrong. See how those edges are crimped up unevenly? Whole thing's probably water-damaged underneath."

We went around to the front of the house, looking for a loose window or something.

"Why in hell is this place locked down like Fort Knox? There's nothing to steal." Thomas's checked agitation bobbed in his speech.

"Oh, the bank thought he was still living out here—he

was, for a little bit there after Caroline made him leave." Josie rattled the latch on my old bedroom window, but it was stuck hard.

"That makes sense. Does anybody know where he is now? He's not here, at least." Thomas was still eyeing every hedge and corner.

I grabbed the old brass handle on the front door, stopping for a second. "We never locked this when I was growing up. Dad always said, if anybody makes it out this far, and they try to get into the house, shoot them."

Thomas allowed as how that might be the one thing they could agree on.

I was almost relieved when the handle wouldn't give, locked up in a way I had never felt it. Suddenly the house felt a lot like somebody else's place. Somebody else's problem. I looked down at the stone front porch, the stoop where I'd sat and closed my eyes so many times hoping to see something else when I opened them. Something besides tobacco and water moccasins.

"The front field. That used to flood real bad."

Josie looked where I pointed. "Oh, yeah, when Aunt Gertrude still lived in the tenant house, she used to talk about the snakes. After y'all took those willows out that used to be over there and put in all that dirt, they didn't come back."

"Snake-free is good."

"There's probably still some snakes. But not the moccasins, I hope. Dad left the tractor out there all spring one time when the motor died in the bottom of the pasture and he said he could see them coming from every direction."

"Did they laugh at him like his smelly witch?"

"Huh. Probably. He was mostly full of bullshit, for sure. There were a few snakes. Probably not taking him and his business all that personally, though."

I clambered through some raggedy azaleas to the living room windows, big panels in the middle with smaller venting panes on the bottom. The living room had been the prettiest room of the house, with a big stone fireplace an old Italian man had built by himself.

"I'd knock this whole thing down and leave just the fireplace," I blurted out. "That stone, it's still beautiful. I remember him—not his name, but I remember the man who built it. His bandana around his neck. The dust all over him. I don't think he spoke a lot of English. One of the first times I realized that Dad could speak another language. At least a little. As far as I know, his Italian mostly allowed him to talk about what to eat and how stupid you were."

"Baby, if we could afford it, we'd buy this house and you and your brother could burn it to the ground and roast marshmallows over it."

My brother Christopher. He'd know about six ways to get into the house if he were here. I didn't grow up with Christopher; I'm about the same age as his mom, in fact. But we shared the same ugly burden of a father, and we both grew up out here in what was rapidly turning into the seventies House of Usher.

Right then, the lower transom window slid out, right into my hands. The knotty old red shag carpet looked faded orange in the sudden daylight. I stuck in my hand and touched it, and it felt cheap, dry, fragile.

I crawled in the narrow window, back thirty years.
Inside, I rolled over and stared up. The wooden ghosts
were still there, hovering over the room, spectral knots in
the pine beams. The big one with the rays of light on its
robe, the princess with a long veil behind her. Every knot
in that ceiling had been a character in my head. The ovals
like indistinct Modigliani faces, tilted at me, asking me,
What are you looking for up here? You have no business
with us. We live on the beam. You live on the ground. Go
away, don't bother us.

"Nicole, are you okay in there? Well, shit. I guess we're
going inside. Let me see if I can fit through Rabbit's hole
here. I swannee. Girl, where'd you get to?" I was glad
Josie and Thomas had hit it off so well. Though Josie was
the most agreeable of personalities, and without a doubt,
Thomas was about as motivated toward general harmony as
I'd ever seen.

Entering the living room felt like being swallowed by the
cavernous, bloated stomach of a dead, dry whale carcass.
The bracing of the ceiling beams, the scenes of so many
childhood narratives acted out by those knot-people,
seemed to curve around me like a great ribcage. I felt the
static and pop in my ears. Not like when a ghost is talking.
Like the beginning of a mild panic attack. Shadows, either
actual or imagined, narrowed my vision like a silent film
transition.

It smelled awful. Mildew, pee, ancient, curdled Winston
cigarette smoke, something vegetative. The carpet was
stained. Even the hearth, the one spot of beauty I remembered, seemed small, like a fourth grader's desk. The cheap
paneling, the clumsy kitchen remodel with stucco made the
room look like a strip mall Mexican restaurant. I couldn't

decide whether or not to be vindicated or deflated by the general shabbiness all around.

Thomas, waist-deep through the window, looked up. Josie was already standing inside, squinting and scrunching her nose.

"Whew! My goodness. It could use some airing."

"Oh God. Oh, I mean. I'm sorry. This is not what I pictured, after your mother..." Thomas dusted his knees and stood straight, scanning the room.

"Mom tends to talk it up a little. She did design it. Well, the original house. It doesn't really look the same now."

But I couldn't say exactly what was different. It used to be an impressive house. The farm kids at my elementary school thought I was rich. One little girl on my bus asked me if I was a princess. I started to cry, because I thought she was making fun of me. I knew I was way too ugly to be a princess.

Back in 1970 there were no McMansions, no "great" rooms with soaring ceilings. My friends mostly lived in trailers, tenant houses, or two-bedroom tract houses in suburbs called Camelot and Heather Hills. Heather Hills was a classy subdivision—it was practically all the way to Garner, and it had a pool.

The center beam, twelve feet above us, hung low like a drooping circus tent. It just didn't seem that impressive anymore. How could our enormous Christmas trees have fit into this tiny room? It was not helping, too, that every subsequent house my mother had lived in since this one had possessed increasingly dramatic ceilings. This room could fit inside her current living room and easily clear the bottom of the second-floor balcony. She had made certain none of us would ever miss this place.

Just as I was starting to feel a little sorry for it, I heard Thomas making some distinctly unhappy sounds.

"Yeah?"

"The floor. You see it?"

I looked, and then I saw the giant warp in the floor alongside the wall, a distortion like a wave dropping into the middle of the room. I nodded, making a slow undulation with my hand.

"There's no crawl space. No way to get to the 1970 plumbing without tearing out concrete. Now this damage— this is probably foundational. Nic, if this place were a car, I think it might be totaled."

Totaled. Yes. This whole house was totaled.

CHAPTER SIX

WE CUT THROUGH LUCINDA'S YARD on the way back to
Josie's house. Edgar, Nora and Lucinda were sitting in
metal garden chairs out back by the bird bath. Edgar had
hold of a good-sized milk-white cat, who had taken up
residence in his lap, looking up from time to time if the
petting became inattentive. A cotton ball paw gave him
a gentle slap if he scratched too close to the question-
mark tail. When we tromped around the bushes, the cat
stretched, shifted, and stared me down.

"Hoo lawd. Whatcha think of your old house there,
Nicky?" Lucinda smiled. She picked up a child's beach toy
plastic bucket from next to the bird bath and waved it at
us. "Y'all see the scuppernongs over there? The arbor's
right where it used to be, remember? Nicole, you and Josie
and Dina and Carrie and Charlie used to lay up under
that thing. Scuse me, Charlotte, I mean. And Caroline.
Y'all would lay there and eat 'em til you threw up. Nora,
take this bucket and go get your mama some of them
scuppernongs."

Nora looked at me, a little desperately.

"Grapes, Nora. Big fat grapes. On that wooden thing
over there at the edge of the field, just before the fence..."

"Oh! I see it. Can you eat them?"

"You can."

Nora chuckled. "I won't throw up. I promise."

"Your problem," I called out.

I sat down in Nora's seat, between Edgar and Lucinda.

Lucinda twisted up the edge of her long white duster, smiling that weird Mona Lisa thing all the women in this family have got going.

"Well?"

"Well. It's not exactly like I remember it. But he's gone, at least."

"Feels different, don't it?"

"Better. Not... regular. But better."

"Sure would be nice to have you out here. Would have made your Granny so happy, seeing you happy like you are now."

"Oh, she wouldn't care a thing about me being out here."

"No. No, that's true. She'd just be glad you're happy."

"She told me once that she was worried I'd die old and alone."

Lucinda laughed so hard it made Edgar jump, and the cat jumped. Upset the little tin table and sent some playing cards flying. I hadn't noticed the cards until then.

"There ain't no chance of that out here, honey. You got Caroline up there, Beth down the path over there, Dina's right where she's always been, you know that and Josie's right here next to ME!" She leaned toward me and pulled my forehead to hers, then let me go with a smile.

"What do you think, Edgar? You want to live in the wooooods?" Edgar liked to say the O part in "woods" really long and mournful, like an owl. I did, too.

"Yes." Edgar held his arms apart and waited for the cat

to make up her mind. She did. Hopped up next to him this time and head-butted his shoulder. *Mine*, said the cat. "Not the house with the monsters."

"Monster?" Edgar had been watching a lot of *Star Wars* and playing a lot of Angry Birds, so I played along. "Is it Chuck?" Chuck was some kind of cranky bluebird. Edgar liked to pretend he was Chuck.

"Monsters. Not Chuck." He shot me a look of disdain. "The monsters in the black capes."

Lucinda didn't turn around. It's not important, I thought.

"What do they look like, Edgar?" Don't ask, I thought, but I asked. Oh my.

"Nothing."

"Okay. That's enough of that." Thomas and Nora came up behind me with a bucket of scuppernongs. I could smell the mustiness and it still made me queasy.

Chapter Seven

It's not that I started collecting old photos. But they did seem to turn up. First there was the shoebox of old family photos I found when Christopher and I decided to get our stuff out of the garage attic at the old house.

"Is that Dad?"

"No—that's *his* Dad..." I started to explain to Christopher. We never got to be actual kids together, but it's only once in a while now that we have to realize that part.

"No, I know—I mean the little *kid*, the one in the birthday hat."

He was right; it was our father. He was recoiling from being placed on a donkey or Shetland pony, clinging to his father, whose cigarette dangled forever on the deckled edge of a fading image, drooping with ash.

There wasn't much worth keeping in the attic. The decrepit Christmas tree stand shaped like a house my grandparents once lived in. A box of kids' books neither of us recognized. My mom's wedding album.

"I told you that train was long gone. Man, after the first couple of episodes of *Pawn Stars,* he sold everything."

"Yeah. I bet that was just a joy to watch. Let me guess: you were all going to be rich."

"As Rockefellers. You bet. I don't even know if he sold it, really. But he took it someplace. Hand me that flashlight, would you?" Christopher reached for the big Maglite I had, but the beam caught a familiar shape.

"What's that—oh, man. *Stratego*. There's a terror from the past."

"Oh, shit," Christopher said, crawling into the path of the flashlight and retrieving the box. "It is *Stratego*. I thought I threw this in a lake or something. I planned to, anyway."

"He made you play, too?" I laughed, but like many of our parallel memories, it was only funny now that we could talk about it.

"There was a phase, yes."

"Before Gin and after *Monopoly*. Yeah. He get mad when you beat him?"

"Fuck, he *beat* me when I beat him."

We sat in the dark for a second, staring down the old dusty box like it was at fault.

"The worst he beat me," I began, "was the night he figured out I let him win."

Christopher let out a low whistle. "How'd he figure it out? I mean, good plan, but..."

"Yeah, not bad for a ten-year-old. My execution was pretty poor, though. I tried to move the flag when he wasn't looking—at first he thought I was cheating, and he was so excited. He thought that's how I was winning. Then he realized I'd intentionally put the flag where he guessed. To be honest, it was the third game we'd played in a row, I was sleepy, and he wouldn't let me go to bed until he won."

"You got to go to bed then, at least."

"Yeah," I sighed, "it was kind of worth getting punched to get to leave the room."

We poked around up there until the pink fur of the insulation started making us itchy, then we clambered down the foldout ladder carrying a handful of pictures, an old Easter basket, a box of Legos, *Stratego* and some more board games.

"*Aggravation?* Who'd play something called that?" Thomas scrutinized the box cover.

"Would you prefer... this?" I held up *Perfection.* "This one I'm pretty sure figures into my current panic disorder triggers. You had sixty seconds to put these geometric pieces in the appropriate holes, and then the box blew the whole table up at you, throwing the pieces in the air."

"That sounds fucking awesome," Christopher smiled a little sadly at me, and Thomas lit cigarettes for both of them as we stood in the threshold of the side door to the garage. I picked away at the splintered wood in the door jamb. A little earlier, Christopher and I had been unable to coax open the pretty solid lock the bank folks had seen fit to place on the garage door. So we picked up an old maul that was still lying on the ground over by the tractor, and we took turns busting the thing down.

"And that, ladies and gentlemen," Thomas said pulling out the board I'd been tearing at, lost in thought, "was the highlight of my afternoon, watching the two of you bust the hell out of that door. I still don't like this place."

Christopher and I split up the photos. I kept one of Granny sitting on an iron bench, her legs slung to the side, ankles crossed. The drape of her gray dress swooped down to touch the grass. Well, it was gray in the black and white picture. It's funny how the past—anything farther back than your parents—all plays out like a black and white movie. What if the colors had all been garish? Would it all seem as charming if that dress was really a heinous orange?

Nora and I spend a lot of time looking through various Internet photo archives. I almost find other people's ancestors easier to manage than my own, though I still get a whiff of their drama, too. But I figure if I can learn to manage their stories when they come to me in places, I can manage the narratives that come to me in pictures. It might have been smarter to think, earlier on, about what I might be inviting. I don't know that there's any use in bringing that up now. I'm just saying.

So this one photo, I kept seeing it. I guess it's pretty popular on the archive pages, and it is a pretty good photo. The third time I came across it, I did what I typically do and pasted it to my Facebook page. You'd respond to it, too—anybody would, her level stare is pretty obviously defiant, hand on her hip. One version was the full frame, three friends similarly dressed on either side. Teddy Girls, that's what they were called. Somewhere in an industrial town in the north of England, 1950s. I found a whole archive page documenting these teenagers, and I was particularly entertained by the sign posted at a dance hall reading "No One Wearing Edwardian Dress Admitted." Who knew the Edwardians were such troublemakers. It was a new world.

The punk rock kids I hung out with in high school used to talk about Teddy Boys and Teddy Girls, but later versions, and a lot of what we knew was wrapped in the propaganda spread around that the groups were racist mobs, violent and out of control. Some of that reputation was rooted in the fear the grownups had for these oddball kids and their probably false sophistication. The clothes, like a cross between Mary Poppins and a rogue Japanese designer from the eighties. Their movie-still poses. How'd they come up with this narrative? Who were they telling the story to? Was there even a narrative, or just these photos, the suggestion of a meaning on one side or the other, but only the suggestion? A life so limited in possibility that the edges of a celluloid box bordered all the drama that would ever be offered.

The photo had captured her, but like on a stage, not like in a cage. When she stared out at me, it was as if she had just done… something. *What are you going to do about it?* What will she do next? Nothing. Just this. Just this looking at you, right now. *You, person in the future. I'm looking at you. I see you.*

"Stand less straight… put your hand in your pocket. No, the other hand." Nora looked at me over the top of the camera and tilted her head sideways.

"What?"

"That's the expression, that, exactly." Then she disappeared behind the black box again.

Nora got serious about photography last year and was up for all kinds of projects. It was my idea to recreate the photo, but she took it all very seriously. By the time we were standing in the yard, I was thinking, maybe I've gotten a little too close to the girl in the photo, trying to put myself in her picture. My jacket wasn't quite the right period, but the photos Nora took did have a very similar feel. I was uncomfortable seeing myself in them later. I felt like an imposter. I *was.*

I didn't know how to research her identity, but I figured if I just kept her photo close, we could be friends at least. You know, this whole process is not far from how I meet real people. Either it works or it doesn't, but it's all I've got. It's hard to work it so that it doesn't freak people out.

Girl in the Picture. I can't keep calling you that. But I'm not sure what your name is. Are you a Pat or a Tricia? An Elizabeth? Because then you can be Eliza (flowers) or Beth or Bess (geometric) or Liz or Lizzie (whatever Trish is). You're not any of those, though.

There's a pin on her lapel I can barely make out. It looks like my mother's sorority pin. Mom never went to college, but evidently if you were a southern woman in the sixties and seventies, you could join a civic sorority, which she did. They did things like send care packages to soldiers in Vietnam, collect for Easter Seals and the March of Dimes, raffle the occasional ham. On the days when Mom went to the meeting, she'd wear the little pin on her shoulder. I can particularly remember a form fitting, orange wool dress—it must have been a favorite of hers to wear to the meetings, because whenever I think of the pin, I think of that dress, and the Pucci-like print scarf tied to the side around her neck.

This girl, the Teddy Girl. She has some asymmetry going on, too, her curls pushed over the left side of her forehead like the droop of a pompadour. Like my mother, she balanced that sweep with the tiny pin on her right side. I check the copy I have of the wider view of the picture, the one with the three other girls in it. No, I don't see the pin on any of them. But two of them have a neck scarf tied just like my mom did, one end tossed jauntily behind the shoulder, one curled toward the face. One of the scarf girls was laughing, her head thrown back, chin out. She was a Margaret. Of some kind. But the middle one, her shoulders squared, her pin shining. She was not. She was a J name.

I think, until I know better, she might be a *Justine.*

Chapter Eight

IT HAD BEEN A WHILE since I'd had what we sometimes have taken to calling "messages from out of town." No narratives slipping into my pocket like the notes that would appear in my apron during my cocktail waitress days. In fact, I'd been going out a little more, getting mighty brave visiting the family land on a regular basis now, and it hadn't been churning up much more than my own sketchy past. So one night when Thomas asked if I wanted to go last-minute to see Ian Hunter, who was playing over in Durham, I violated six or eight of my usual items on the "situations to avoid" list. Last minute plans. Crowded bars. School night outings. And, chiefly, the Durham Ware-house district, which was mega-haunted. You'll just have to trust me. Hauntville.

"Hey, that guy you said you wanted to go see is tonight."

"Which guy?"

"The old one." Our musical tastes overlap, but Thomas has got a higher tolerance for contemporary country, a broader knowledge of jazz, and evidently I'm just pretty old.

Columbia is the biggest bar in the warehouse district, near the old baseball park. A bunch of these old buildings in Durham are renovated, and from those I don't usually get much input. Like the Carolina Theater—that place had some aggressive, angry energy upstairs until they gutted the thing and it's gone, that sparkly, hazy balcony floor. All those hoarse whispers echoing around up there. Somebody told me it had been a popular place to shoot heroin in the seventies, and I guess it's no big leap to think that those faint silvery slivers I could almost see in the corners of ladies' room might have been trying to find their way home in the dark.

Thomas had gotten us maneuvered into the edge of the main room crowd, past the bar lines. I wasn't even grabbing his elbow yet, not a bit panicked. I was checking out the room, and I knew pretty soon Thomas would notice that he might well be the youngest person in the audience. Eighties bands favored by record store boys are my weakness. Thomas goes along.

"He's busting out the hits early!" Thomas yelled in my ear as "Once Bitten, Twice Shy" cranked up, only two songs into his set.

"Man, I think Coldwater Creek rose up and flooded this place." There was a woman next to us in a watercolor sweater, doing a butterfly hippie dance. "You've got to admit, though, it's pretty hopeful, seeing this many old people rockin' out."

Thomas looked up for a second, doing some kind of math in his head. "If you say so, baby."

One time I had this dream where I was really old and in a retirement home and my friend Rick, who cuts my hair, was with me. It was lunchtime on Tuesday, and it said so on a big poster in the cafeteria. It also said it was haircut time, and Rick was shaving mohawks and wrapping people's little old heads up in shower caps full of dye. All the old people had neon shanks of whatever hair they had left. And Hüsker Dü poured out of the speakers by the buffet table. It was kind of a good dream.

Anyway, this place. This bar. If only we had Rick to shave some mohawks and liven it up a little. The point is, the crowd wasn't rowdy or pushy, all was well, a little too well for a rock show, you know? And then all of a sudden I realized I wasn't breathing. I mean, I was physically breathing, but no air was coming in. I held my head up, thinking maybe the crowd was getting to me, maybe I just needed some air from a little higher up, a breeze. I did that square-breathing thing again that my yoga teacher taught me. Nothing. I felt like my face was filling up with something. My chest felt crushed.

"I'm going to the bathroom," I pulled Thomas's jacket sleeve down like a bus stop line and walked past him. He nodded, gave me a little squint to see if I was really okay. It was pretty easy to get to the hallway for the rest rooms since it was a slow song and the crowd was even looser than earlier, clusters moving back toward the bar. There was a young kid at the pedestal in the hallway checking IDs and hand stamps. He seemed to be doing some kind of homework on an iPad, clicking on multiple choice answers. Maybe he was just taking a Buzzfeed quiz. He glanced up at me as I took off my jacket and stood there for a minute. I was fine. I could even hear the little beeps of his device—wrong answers?—his expression stayed flat as he made choice after choice, only brief seconds of consideration for each.

In the hallway, I was better almost immediately, so I felt a little silly hiding around the corner while I could hear the band starting into "Sweet Jane." So I wheeled around and went back in, dodging bodies, until I found Thomas right where I left him.

"That was fast!" he yelled into my ear as I tackled him lightly around the waist. All of a sudden, my knees buckled and a rushing noise filled my ears. My cheeks were burning and the music sounded all jumbled up. I didn't know if I could make it back to the hallway.

"And just as fast you were gone," Thomas said later, in the inevitable debriefing that follows these episodes.

In the hallway again, it was like coming up for air from the deep end of the swimming pool. My lungs filled up, to my relief, and the rushing stopped. All good. A quick nod from the kid at the pedestal, and I backed up and into the main room, heading toward the stage.

The third time I took off, Thomas was only mildly paying attention. I know it sounds disorganized, but we've got signals worked out for this sort of thing now.

Back in the hallway one more time, the kid with his iPad glanced up for an impatient second. I figured I was most likely exhibiting some kind of red-flag behavior, but he didn't look like somebody who'd be too protocol-obsessed. Of course, if he was the one who'd have to come with the bucket later, it'd be in his best interest to stay sharp.

"Hey, ma'am,"

Damn, I hate it when they call me ma'am.

"*What?*" Irritated, but I guess I understood why he might be bothered. "Don't worry; I'm not going to throw up."

"Yeah. Because the bathroom—"

"I see it. I'm good. I just need a second." It took a little longer this time to bounce back, just because it did sort of feel like panic attack territory. The kid looked over the podium, his chin fuzz lit up with iPad glow. He looked too young to have grown facial hair, especially with that facial expression. How could you not be used to drunks and weirdos in that job? Who puts a skinny, ill-equipped fellow like this in a dark hallway watching for bad behavior? He needs somebody to walk him to his car, for fuck's sake.

All of a sudden, he hopped off the barstool and fled. Seemed like both a moment of admirable self-preservation and overreaction. But before I could even look up again, he was back with a little plastic cup of bubbly water.

"Hey, drink something. It's just club soda. It's okay."

"Thanks." I took the cup and downed it. I realized my forehead was damp. I'd felt trapped. The club soda felt freezing cold in my throat but scratched and burned when I swallowed. But it hit some kind of reset button and my breathing went completely back to normal, the magic power of carbonation. The music had stopped at some point. The only sounds were some shuffling and tuning, the low *rutabaga-rhubarb* hushed crowd sounds. I had sunk down to the floor, where things looked pretty squalid. He crouched next to me.

"I have anxiety, too. Right? Panic attack?" The kid's flat expression persisted when he made the pronouncement, but his eyebrows raised up a little.

"Oh yeah, I know." I said. "But these aren't mine. These feelings." I sure didn't want to be ungrateful, though, so I tried to smile as I straightened myself back up. "I'm okay now. You should call your grandmother, by the way. The one in the yellow house. Thanks for the water." I handed him the cup and went back into the bar.

I found Thomas immediately. He'd moved to a completely different location, halfway back to the bar near the big recycling cans.

"Had to take a phone call?" He smiled. Like I said, we have signals worked out.

"Something along those lines."

Thomas is my third husband. He's always seemed to have good sense about the fact that I'll talk about it when I *can*—that's a chief reason I won't be running away again.

I can't always confirm or refute the experiences I have, of course. Those two girls I met on Morrow Mountain when Thomas and I first started trying to put a name to what I have—the fact that I could prove who they were, find their names—that made the whole incident an outlier, an anomaly. Usually I just have to trust what I feel and try to narrate it to myself as best I can. So don't think it's too wrong of me when I tell you I felt better when I read later about the fire there. That whole district used to be industrial, machine shops, factories. Lots of accidents. The place where Columbia stands today had been a tool and die shop. The fire was in the 30s, workers trapped in the building, couple of casualties, one death. I told you—a lot of bad things happened in Durham. It's way haunted up in there.

There are so many bad things in the world that don't make any sense. I think it's marginally better when at least they make sense. You can blame me for that if you want.

Chapter Nine

I can't say they are nightmares, but ever since the photo experiments started, I've had darker dreams. The one with the figures in the hallway, that one was a nightmare. But the one last night was special. The Contessa di Castiglione singing the Dead Weather cover of "New Pony" startled and exhilarated me. Of course that's what she'd be doing if she were around these days. Wearing that mask, tossing her hair. Singing with Jack White.

"The Who-di-What?" I've exceeded the number of random references and connections a conversation can bear, and Thomas lets me know.

"You remember the lady I told you about? In the pictures?"

"The one you dressed up as?"

"No, but I would. I haven't yet. The Contessa di Castiglione—she was—how to explain? I guess her art form was the selfie. All her life, she orchestrated these elaborate tableaux to have herself photographed in all kinds of bizarre contexts." I pulled up the file on my phone where I kept all the photos I'd found so far and showed the first one to Thomas.

"Nineteenth century glamor shots."

"More like... well, maybe. If you mean glamor in the widest sense. Look, here she is with a raven."

"Whoa. What's going on in this one? Looks like she's some kind of Aztec divinity."

"I think she invented her own cosmology and history in

here. Not sure it corresponds to anything actual. Here's the one with the mask."

"Oh yeah, you showed me this one. So that's what she looked like in your dream?"

"Yeah, except that she was dancing kind of like that guy from Future Islands crossed with Tina Turner. Bellowing at me."

"Well?"

"Well?" I wasn't sure there was enough sense in this whole story to keep telling it to Thomas, but he did seem committed to making it make sense.

"How long have you been looking at her pictures? Think she's trying to tell you anything?"

The short answer was *Yes*. Because this woman is trying to tell everybody a lot in these pictures. Nothing could be any clearer than that.

I thought about it before I answered, though. "I don't know. When we were looking at the pictures before, I didn't know the people, and my impressions were pretty quick. I've been friends with the Countess here for some time. I'd think if we were going to party together, it would have happened by now."

"Sounds like it maybe did last night." He had a point.

I reconsidered the dream, turned it around in my memory. The Countess, Jack White, I couldn't see the rest of the audience. Was there an audience? I couldn't see the rest of the audience, just the stage. Something about voodoo... *your feet walk by themselves.* I hadn't been able to look away when she pointed at me.

Besides, I could pretend like Thomas's suggestion was an unlikely one, but I had been doing my best for weeks to hear from Justine, the real "girl in the picture" for me these days. My first impression from the photo was the desire to step into that scene and live there for a little while.

After I found I could get things from photos, I started looking at Facebook pages of missing people. I didn't tell anybody about it. Probably from fear of seeming creepy. But I guess I thought maybe I could help. I kept a record for a few weeks, just checking to see if I could establish whether or not the stories I got could actually help somebody. That's what I was looking for, after all. A way to help.

But almost immediately, it got to be too much. The first one turned out to be a young man with Aspergers—they didn't say so until they found him, but I knew it when I saw his last Facebook post. I could see his frustration and his sense of purpose. He left on a mission, and I felt certain he was okay. He showed up later, two states away, having left home one afternoon to go visit a friend with whom he'd had some sort of altercation. He'd wanted to resolve it in person.

The next girl had been mad at her step mother. And they also found her safe, with a friend I had seen as her traveling partner. So far, so good. But the third one—I was still right about the anxiety, the loneliness. But my oddly vague sense that she was safe turned out to be wishful thinking. I stopped looking at the missing people pictures. I had to turn it off. I still hadn't mentioned any of this to Thomas, but I would. Someday. It seemed only fair to include the data.

"I also woke up hungry for a very specific food that I can't have." This part was easier to explain, a little. It's easier to explain absence than it is to explain loss. Though they are, as a great poet once explained to me, crossed boulevards in cheap-shot city. One day I'd tell Thomas about the missing people. But it was easier to talk about food.

"Ah."

I stared at him for a minute or two, but he didn't even look up.

"Aren't you going to ask me what specific food?"

"Oh! I totally thought that was a metaphor for something."

"No. An actual food, and I can't possibly have it, because the place it's from is far away and might not be there anymore."

"Turkish Delight from Narnia?"

"What? No. Plus you can get Turkish Delight. I bet Amazon's got two-hour shipping on that stuff."

Thomas waved off my suggestion and made a squinchy face. "Yeah, but in the book it sounds like something great, and in real life it's disgusting. What kid eats dried fruit in sawdust?"

"I actually like Turkish Delight, for your information. But that's not what I'm talking about. I want a cheese Danish from Suzy's Diner."

"All you want is a cheese Danish? Baby, we can get you a cheese Danish."

"Not just any cheese Danish. I don't know why it's—

maybe it was the cold air smell this morning, and I remembered working at the bookstore in Atlanta, walking in the morning down to Suzy's, the diner in my neighborhood. Suzy used to get these big cardboard trays of cafeteria cheese Danishes, the really flat ones with the diagonal white sugar frosting lines."

"Mmmm." Thomas smacked his lips, but I kept going.

"No wait; I'm not done."

"I'm not really being facetious. I like a crappy cheese Danish out of a vending machine."

"Oh gosh—that's exactly what they were. The vending machine kind. Now I get it—they're in the same spot in my brain reserved for old school Zingers. The anti-Twinkies. You can't get those now, either. Maybe there's a tasty, carcinogenic yellow food dye that fell out of use in the last twenty years. Anyway, the best part of the Suzy's cheese Danish..."

"There's really more? Because you had me at 'diagonal white sugar frosting lines'."

"Suzy would toss one out of the cardboard tray like a Frisbee over to the griddle. It'd slide until it hit a bank of hashbrowns or bacon cooking, and she'd leave it there a few seconds and then BLAM! Smack it with the spatula."

"Hot damn."

"That's what I mean. She'd flatten it on the one side, let it sizzle for a minute, then flip it over. She'd squash it again, you'd see the little bubbles popping in the butter, and after about twenty seconds she'd flip it up with the spatula onto a little white paper plate, one of those pleated ones like a collar on a little girl's dress."

"I have seen such plates."

"Yes. They are diner-ubiquitous. Anyway: plastic wrap, cardboard, yellow dye, frosting zigzags, butter tinged with bacon and hashbrowns and ham and eggs and onions sometimes or whatever else had visited the griddle that day. The rap of Suzy's righteous spatula. Being so screeching hungry because I ate ramen noodles the last three nights in the house I shared with a band and four cats. And it was cold, or just starting to be. And I worked in a bookstore."

"I see."

"Yes."

"And you were in love."

"Always. But no, not really. I did love Suzy, though. She was a solid woman."

"Ate a lot of cheese Danishes?"

"No, I mean she was—"

I got lost in the geography of what was turning out to be a pretty good story. I could see Suzy in my head the time I came to visit her last, about ten years ago. I was only in Atlanta for a few days, but I went to see if the diner was still there. It was, but her son was running the place. He'd only been a teenager when I used to come there for breakfast every day.

"I'll call Mom—she'll want to see you." I can't remember his name for the life of me. He was trying to be a rapper, and all I can remember are a series of tentative rap handles. L-Ray. Ray-D, Ray Gun. Had his name been Ray? Maybe.

She did remember me, it turned out. I couldn't believe it. I asked about her daughter, her grandchildren. Back

then, I went down one day with Suzy to court when she had
to have a witness to talk to Child Protective Services with her.
The daughter was going through a bad time, Suzy didn't want
the kids in foster homes. It was a mess, but Suzy just needed
somebody to vouch for her. I knew where she was every
morning. I watched her cook eggs for what seemed like every
construction worker in Atlanta. And in the early nineties,
that was a freaking lot of construction workers. She let the
homeless guy who dressed in a business suit and talked about
himself in third person ("He only wants a cigarette") take the
trash out and she'd give him a ham biscuit. He'd take it apart
and talk to it for a while before he ate it. Sometimes he'd
arrange parts of it on the sidewalk and leave it there, though.
That's all you can do.

It didn't seem like it had been all that long, but so much
had changed, and in all the predictable ways. L-Ray was a
little stiff with me, the way you would be with someone you
assumed still thought of you as a kid. "I'm taking care of
things now," he seemed to say every time he straightened
the menus or opened the register. The daughter was gone.
No one had details. The grandchildren, a handful. Smart
but bored in school. *I'm too old to raise more kids,* Suzy said. Her
husband had been dead for years; it must have happened
right after I left.

That day broke my heart. I missed her fearlessness so
much. How selfish was that, though? To miss the Suzy I
knew, like I even had a Suzy of my own, separate, like a photo
in a locket? All that Suzy had known of me was that I was a
shuffling, music-scene, fake-poet, little girl who sat every
morning at her counter drinking free refills and eating
nothing but a goddamn Danish. Praying I'd be long gone
before the rent went up. I was.

Thomas's voice called me back twenty years and 400 miles.

"You ought to dress up like the Countess di Whatever. Halloween's coming."

"Who? Oh. Every day was Halloween for her. Hm. Maybe. I could make a frame to wear."

"Because that, surely, would make it clear to everyone who you were."

"Surely it would. I'd be the Lady in the Picture. That's all anybody needs to know."

The lady's coming out of the picture these days, just a little bit.

...pray to that God you're praying to...

Countess, what you want from me? I see you. What's your business with me? I'm a liar and a fraud. I'm using voodoo. My feet walk by themselves.

CHAPTER TEN

"I'm still trying to decide if it's a good idea."

The experiments continued. Despite all common sense reasons not to, we were spending the night on the property, all of us.

Thomas waved a handful of tent stakes at me. "Decide fast, because the sun's going down and the tent is going up. By the way, if you're going to stand there blocking what's left of the light, why don't you hold these?"

"I mean, before we go any further, I know I've got to figure out whether or not I can live out here. And I'm not sleeping in *there*—" I pointed up the hill to the house I grew up in, slumped and stretched out in the dusk like the party guest who drank too many Harvey Wallbangers.

"I do think something might have died in there. Don't hurt yourself, but can you hand me another one?"

"Thomas, I'm admiring your efficiency with the mallet. If I'd been that efficient with a mallet, my whole life trajectory would have been different."

"Maximum-security prison."

"Not necessarily. I might have been an international champion or something."

"At what? Whack-A-Mole?"

"I don't know. Don't most sports involve hitting things?"

"Not with a mallet."

"You're splitting hairs."

"You're darting around like a water bug. Look, once this tent is up, I'm camping out here tonight. Are you decided? Don't decide by not deciding, please. That never works out well for the rest of us."

I saw Edgar following Nora with a forked twig. Her gestures suggested she might be trying to explain to him how to dowse for water.

"Are you laughing? I'm not sure it's funny yet, so please tell me what you're laughing at."

"I'm laughing at our strange and wonderful children. Alright, I'm aiming to be fine. I can't bear to tell them they'll have to pack up all these lighting implements. I'm just not sure. Do you think we have enough flashlights and lanterns? What is this device? Does it light up as well?"

"It's a stove. I guess it lights up. But only when you burn wood in it. And there's no such thing as enough flashlights."

"Maybe that was the problem."

I remember as a kid how dark it would get every night. Sundown was the saddest time of day. I'd sit on this exact hill and watch the last little threads of light disappear, and for a split second I'd wonder if I'd ever see daylight again.

"Look, you can see the stars already, even with the sun still hanging on."

"You're right," I said, "The stars."

"Can't see that view in town." Thomas gave two hard smacks to the last tent post. The water shield made the two-room tent look even more impressive, like some kind of clean, orange, geometric transportation module for beings from another planet. Which we kind of were. I used

to walk through the tall pasture grass right here on my way
to the barn, terrified if I'd gotten home late and had to go
down there alone to feed the horses. But it was my job, so
I went. Horses are kind of spooky in the dark. I'm not a
horse person. They're super-needy, like friends who just
broke up with a long-term partner. I think I'd be better off
as a goatherd, should we get out here and decide we need
to farm something. Llamas or something. Something aloof
and judgmental. Or something unruly.

I want to say it was beautiful out there when the sun went
down and the stars turned on one by one over our heads,
like a bunch of other families, far away, clustered around
their own campfires. I want to believe that I thought it was
beautiful that night. Both kids were asleep by our little
fire. I was watching Thomas play Nora's small guitar and
holding my ukulele in my lap. Nora's guitar has a good-
sized sound for a scaled-down instrument, but it looks
kind of funny on Thomas, so he doesn't play it often. I
like the absurdity of the ukulele. It felt like the stakes were
much lower. You're not claiming much musical ability if
all you do is cackle Ramones covers out on a ukulele.

"The only thing that stops you is you can't stand sucking
at anything."

"I'm sorry, but how is that not a valid argument for
restraint?"

"*Everybody* sucked the first time they picked up an instrument. The Ramones sucked when they started playing."

"They sucked with style. That was the point."

"Miles Davis sucked. Elvis sucked."

"I don't believe it. The King did not ever suck. He
was born not sucking. Miles Davis, Elvis, Jerry Lee Lewis,

Louis Armstrong—aliens came to earth and gave them their gifts."

"Aliens. Okay. So you just want to skip mediocre? See, that's a problem. Everybody these days wants to be good without getting good."

"What was that?"

"I said, 'everybody wants to be good without…'"

"No, no—I heard you—what's that other sound over there, past those scrub pines?"

"Man, is it going to be a long night if every rustle in the leaves—"

"Pig!"

"What? That's an ugly thing to—"

"Not you! PIG!" I jumped up so fast the folding chair flew up in the air and landed partway in the campfire. I grabbed Edgar up in the quilt and turned in time to see Thomas with his back to Nora, the feet of the flaming folding chair in his hands. The pig ran at full gallop and at first seemed on a trajectory for Thomas, but seeing the flames it zigzagged, squealing in terror. Between the lanterns on the tent and the giant torch the chair turned out to be, we could see it pretty clearly, its rippling flesh and muddy hooves springing through the edge of the trees.

"Jesus Christ!" Thomas waved the chair trying to extinguish the fire. I knew he'd be looking for the rifle, so I grabbed the keys out of his jacket and popped open the back door of the jeep. The grunts of the pig starting to fade, Thomas sprinted over to the jeep, pulled out the household rifle and disappeared into the trees. Nora was sitting up, slightly bleary. Edgar was still sleeping when the shot cleared some bats, an owl, and something like a rabbit or fox out of the edge of the woods.

"I am oooooo-kaaaay!" Thomas called out from someplace in the dark, past the light of the lanterns and flashlights. Nora held up the big spotlight and we saw him, a little blood on his jacket, pushing branches to the side and stepping over underbrush.

"How about you turn that thing sideways before you burn out my eyeballs."

"Oh, sorry." Nora dropped the angle of the spot, but we could still see him. He came over and cleared the rifle on the open end of the jeep, wiped it down and locked it back away. Nobody said anything for a while.

"I'll call somebody tomorrow." Thomas took off his glasses and rubbed his eyes. "We should get some sleep."

"Is it dead?" Nora asked, in what was, all considered, a pretty steady voice. This kind of thing is not a big deal when you grow up in the country, but Nora didn't grow up in the country. I don't even really claim the authority of having grown up in the country. I never hunted, I never really farmed. I quit 4-H because all the leaders ever did was make out with each other in the barn loft.

"You could see it okay? Think it could have been one of Grady Phillips' pigs?" Josie had told us so much about Grady, who would be our neighbor when we moved. Nothing says "hello" like taking out the neighbor's livestock. I was thinking maybe none of us were cut out for this.

"Yeah, I saw it. There's a clearing on the other side of that stand of trees. I saw him pretty clear under the moon. Nothing anybody could do. Wild pig on a rampage. You gotta take that poor bastard down. If he wasn't wild before, he was acting wild now." That's the thing; Thomas can negotiate the difficult situations. He wasn't a big hunter, but he'd shot his share of squirrels and a few deer. Mostly he knew better than to leave an enraged half-alive wild animal in the woods near where our kids might be playing

We all slept pretty well, considering. First thing the next morning, Grady's truck came rolling over the hill into the old pasture, Josie and Lucinda in the cab up front with Grady, with a big oil drum cooker trailing behind, bumping and swaying over the dips that were what was left of old furrows.

It was the first time we'd met Grady in person, but the introductions were brief so that he and Thomas could go off to retrieve the carcass. Thomas had gone back to check at daylight and returned with the report that he was pretty sure it was no wild boar and must have escaped from Grady's pen, less than a mile through the woods from where we were camped. But when they came out carrying the thing slung in a tarp between them, Grady was smiling and shaking his head.

"Not my pig," Grady said. "At least, not unless it's one that I counted as lost a long time ago. We had an old bobcat out here getting the pigs and chickens—"

I glanced at Nora as her eyes widened and she mouthed "bobcat" very slowly behind her hand toward me.

Grady went on. "That ol' bobcat, sometimes he'd eat a pig or chicken mostly right there, leave a mess so you'd know, but sometimes he'd just take the whole thing with him. You'd not see anything but some feathers or a hoof, maybe."

Nora had sidled up behind me, and at this point she whispered "voodoo bobcat." I waved her off.

"Hadn't heard much out of him in a while, that bobcat. Anyway, I had some little pigs going missing all the time a few years back. This one coulda been mine, living in the woods. They do that. Don't take a pig no time to go wild again."

"Really? I never knew that. I grew up out in Stanly County, and for a while there, they had a real problem across the line in Anson County with the feral pigs."

"That's right. All those wild pigs out there, they just farm pigs that got loose. You can't go looking for every one you lose." He scratched his head for a second, then put his cap back on. A plain cap. Not advertising anything. "Can't say I've seen any in these woods, but I can't say I'd be surprised to find one. Now come to think of it, when I was a little boy, my granddaddy told me there were pigs and some chickens even that lived out deep in these woods that had been there from a long time ago. Back when Sherman came through here, folks hid their livestock in the woods so the Union soldiers wouldn't get 'em. Some of 'em ran off, and some they said were still out there. Your great-grandaddy. He ever talk about that?"

Grady looked at me. I shrugged and shook my head. I'd heard stories, but not about pigs.

"Do you... mark your pigs in some way?" Nora's delight in the mundane macabre was in overdrive, I could see. Grady laughed a little at her question. He had a big landscaping business—the farm was really part entertainment and part nostalgia for him.

"Naw. Never have. Like I said, except for the one spell

of it, I don't lose many. Usually only have about five or six a season. I give two to the Optimist Club every year. They cook one at the Christmas tree lot and raffle off the other one. Last year they sent the Scouts to D.C. Not sure this year—I think they're gonna build a playground in that park over there behind where the Piggly Wiggly used to be..."

Thomas and Grady continued their discussion of club activities. The Optimists met at our friend's restaurant, it turned out. Tuesday nights? Yes, Tuesdays. Thomas's band held practice most Tuesdays, but he was interested. While Grady went on to invite Thomas to participate in this year's Christmas tree lot activities, I inched over closer to the tarp edge. I couldn't tell if I was looking at a snout or a hoof, but a dirty piece of pig poked out from under the black sheeting. I lifted the edge with my boot. Leaning back I almost fell over Nora, who was glued to me. Edgar had moved his tiny folding chair over near the guys so he could follow the conversation, faintly mimicking their hand gestures.

The pig had looked black or dark brown from a distance, but up close in daylight, it seemed like he might be pinky brown. You forget how much pig skin looks like human skin. I don't know; maybe you don't forget. I don't know how much time you spend with pigs.

"Look at his fangs!" Nora knelt down and put a finger on the tip of the pig's incisor.

"That's not a fang, exactly. They're called tusks. I can see you composing a *Weekly World News* headline in your noggin. Vampire Pigs of Piedmont, North Carolina."

"Look at it though."

"That's pretty much what a pig mouth looks like.

They're animals. Don't you watch the *Discovery Channel*? They don't look like Wilbur or Olivia."

"I know, I know." She sat back on the ground next to the carcass. "I guess it really could have hurt us."

"Sure. It's big, heavy, and pointy. Hey, since it was after you, are you going to feast on your enemy later?"

I expected her to snort a refusal. Nora's situational vegetarianism suspended itself on occasion, it was true. And particularly for things like Italian cured meats or bacon. But usually not so much for the visceral. She had a pretty strong aversion to anything that still had bones or a face. But she didn't say anything for a little bit. She just sat there looking stern. Then she got up, brushed off her jeans and walked over to the cooker, examining the gauge and lifting the handle slowly.

"Let's get him going," Grady called out to us all. "He's pretty good size. Really shoulda had him on the cooker before sunup. Supper's gonna be late, but you'll have barbecue for the freezer."

Chapter Eleven

So I decided to go to a psychic convention for rational answers. You heard me. How's that for a plan? It was called something like the 'Head, Heart and Spirit Convention' and it was held at the state fairgrounds. That's what they called it on the website.

A piece of advice: the next thing you don't want to Google, right after anything that sounds like porn, is "psychic" anything. I think diving into the dark seas of the Internet might be worse than random Ouija board conversations with demonic spirits, because there are fake demons online who are actual people sitting in their not-imaginary basements at keyboards messing with other real people they don't know and will never see in real life. And that shit tracks you now, like tiny black helicopters hovering over every keystroke. As of this week, my Gmail ads think I'm a psychic transvestite wearing stripper heels while I hunt bobcats with allergy-prone dogs. Gmail also thinks I need to go back to grad school online. And that I need to meet some Single Men of Faith. Those ads are just like a holiday trip home from college: *You people do not know me at all.*

As soon as I walk into the Jim Graham Agricultural Center, I feel like I shrank down and fell into my old SpinArt set. I wander into the main display hall, trying to find the conference room where the talk I'm trying to attend will be taking place. But it's all like a highly organized Harry Potter episode or something. Cloaks. Glitter. Rainbows, Wings—it's a Stevie Nicks nightmare caught in a crescent moon dreamcatcher. The smells start to overpower me almost immediately. The sage isn't so bad, but the musky cheap oily incense crap and the waves of patchouli make me remember a bad, humid night in a series of New York taxis.

Next to the aural photography booth, I approached a woman with a table full of crystals. "I'm trying to find Conference Room B," I said.

"All the presentations are upstairs," she explained, gesturing past the tables and behind the big blue curtain in back.

"Thanks. Namaste." I gave her a short nod and tried not to look desperate. How had I even found out about this thing? It seemed like a poor idea already, and rapidly devolving. Psychic fair indeed. If this enterprise were going to be worth it at all, there would be some kickass rides. Simulated astral projection. Unicorn pony rides.

Conference Room B was already packed out the door. I couldn't see the woman speaking, but I could hear her voice like a cascade, a northern accent, but not Jersey. Clipped and precise, super fast. I edged along the side of the room until I got to a window sill alcove to lean in. My black pea coat, fashionable everywhere outside this room, made me look like the freaking forces of evil in this room full of angel wings and rainbows. I slumped down and flattened against the window. Because, you know, that kind of behavior makes you look much friendlier.

It was still hard to see her. She wasn't even five feet tall. Maybe 4' 11". She had long, shiny black hair and gypsy coloring, set off by her regalia, multi-colored panels in a wide, circular skirt. She was a tambourine short of a Halloween costume, and for a minute, I kind of gave up. This kind of charade was exactly the sort of thing I feared all these years, the kind of thing that made me want to turn away completely from making any effort to understand what was happening to me, find out if it was rooted in anything real. This roomful of people was not helping.

"She's not—I wish I could help you, but she's not—I'm seeing her as passed. A long time. It's been a long time? Three years? Four years? Honey, she is not alive. I'm sorry."

The cluster of people around her looked Lumbee to me. I'd had quite a few students from down east, some still mostly full Lumbee Indian. That tribe had not assimilated as much as the Cherokee had. All native North Carolinians seemed to have some Cherokee back there someplace, especially if you weren't too rich or precious about it. If you were small town Episcopalian, yeah, maybe you didn't have any Cherokee. Or if you did, it just didn't seem polite, so you pretended otherwise.

She held the older woman's hand a long time, said some things to her I had to be closer to hear. Pretty soon she walked up to a table at the front of the room.

"Okay, here's how this is going to go. I'm going to talk for about fifteen minutes about what I do, and then we're going to get to these questions you all have for me."

This part—that's the reason I came. When I read about this woman, the article described her as a historical medium. I'd never seen anybody characterized quite that way before, so I kept reading. She had done "site work," visiting archaeological digs to help pinpoint locations.

It was pretty interesting. She rambled a little at the beginning, some stuff about driving back and forth to work while she was staying someplace while her house was being painted and possibly cleared of some unhappy spirits, and on her irregular route, she was daily distracted by an old farm house set far away from the road. We all see old farm houses beside the road every day. They don't all seem to move and speak to us. But some of us see that kind of thing. It happens. I wondered if anyone else was listening to her because it happens to them. I really hoped so. I couldn't tell. All I knew was that the room, for all its rainbows and angel wings, was full of bad dreams. Broken things. Demands. Everyone in the room wanted something from her. I watched her talk about the house, how she got increasingly excited every day to see it. The people in this room were all thinking, *I don't care about your house.* Did she know? Maybe. She held up one finger every so often. Be patient. Be patient. I'm telling you something important.

"So my husband finally says, 'Get in the car.'"

I thought to myself, that's exactly what Thomas would say. That's exactly what Thomas would do. They drove down the dirt road to get to the old house, she told us, and it was even bigger and older, the closer they got. She got out of the car and walked, she said, even faster than her big, tall husband, striding as hard as she could on her tiny legs across the tall grass and spongy ground toward the front of the house, which was oriented away from the modern road, a road that had not existed when the house was built. Then she saw the people.

She was a good storyteller, because yeah, when she said, "Then I saw them, standing out there in the front yard," a big old chill went up my spine and I was waiting for the news, the information, whether or not her husband saw them, too. Not if they were real. I knew they were real. I just wanted to know if they were still alive.

Turns out they were. They were researchers from the

history department at the University of North Carolina at
Wilmington. They were excavating parts of the grounds in
order to document the locations of the family cemetery,
which they had pretty much secured. Markers and fence
lines had survived. They had some diary information,
however, that a slave cemetery existed on the property
as well. Unmarked, of course. Some previous digs had
not revealed anything, though, and the researchers were
plotting their steps again from the main house to the
original kitchen, what may have been the original kitchen,
from which they hoped to pace out the location of the
cemetery. They were on the last try with the information they had. Maybe the diaries were inaccurate. Maybe
this wasn't the site of the original kitchen. All this the
researchers explained to the tiny, bejeweled, energetic,
gypsy-like lady. I had a pretty good picture in my head
of what this whole exchange might have looked like, and
I wished for not the first time in my life that what I had
actually set out to do was make movies. She was great, this
lady, at telling a story.

Micky was her name. By the time she explained to the
researchers her interest in the house, her daily commu-
nion with it, either her compelling use of narrative or
their sheer desperation and lack of further ideas to pursue
induced them to allow her into the house. Inside, Micky
"met" a slave woman. The cook. They got to talking. They
talked a long time. Micky said the woman had been lonely
in the house. She was fairly young, an animated, energetic
figure, and she took Micky through the rooms of the house
and pointed out where everything used to be—the kitchen
work table, the wash stand, the bench to take your boots
on and off. In an hour or so, Micky emerged. She walked,
slowly this time, out to the edge of the woods behind the

house and turned sharply away from the area where the researchers had been digging. Tearfully, she pointed to a rough patch of ground covered in young pines.

They found the cemetery there a few days later. What Micky didn't tell the people was that the cook had walked her to the trees and pointed out the spot where her own baby had been buried when it was born too soon and its lungs failed to fill. She told Micky that even though they buried her son among the slaves, he had never been one.

I didn't know about Micky, but her whole story kind of wore me out. At the same time it made me a little excited, too. I wondered about being able to do something that decisive. I mean, I was really impressed, because it seemed totally plausible to me. Her description of the young cook reminded me a lot of the girl I met in Paul Revere's house in Boston who tried to stop me from jumping out the "window" that had been made into a rear exit when the house had been converted into a historical site. When Micky opened up for questions, I was a little disappointed. I really wanted to hear more about her. I hadn't lost anybody, though. This room was full of people with practical concerns, and I understood that. It was just so disheartening to hear her say the same speech over and over. Heartbreaking.

"I'm just—I'm not hearing—the voice, if I'm hearing it, you understand, it's a voice that has passed. I'm sorry, honey. I know it's not the news—there, there. I'm sorry."

Good lord, I thought, I cannot fathom how this woman does this kind of thing on a regular basis. First of all, you don't need a psychic to tell you, if you haven't seen your baby sister in eight and a half years since she was going to stop at the ATM machine on the way to your house, that she is probably not alive.

You don't need a psychic to tell you it might have something to do with her boyfriend that beat up on her. You don't need a psychic to say that a body of water might be involved. Or the woods. Something.

"I'm sorry, everybody. I have a kind of—well, she's, this one, heh." Micky tilted her head to one side and put a hand on her opposite hip. Then she folded her arms and shook her head. "This one is a pistol. Lady, you just wait, would you?"

Micky walked over to the far side of the crowd and talked to some people on the front row about a girl in a white dress. "No, honey; she's much older. I mean she's young, but she lived a long time ago. I can't always predict who's going to talk. She's got something to say, what can I say? She's... do you have an aunt? Great-aunt? It's her sister. There was an accident. Well, I'm telling you. You may not know, but she knows. She's telling us. She's telling us right now."

She crossed back to the center of the room and scanned the crowd, which was getting increasingly distressed. Even I could tell that. I was starting to wish I could open the window next to me, but I doubted that would go over very well. "We think we know what to ask our loved ones. We think we know what we're missing. We don't know. What they know is far better than anything we can even conceive of—how could we possibly know what to ask them? What we think is important may be completely trivial to them. This isn't bad news, you have to understand." She emphasized the *have to*—she talked to the audience like she had lined up her own children to tell them not to play in the street or get into a stranger's van.

"I want you to think about what I'm saying. I want you

to take this out of here with you. We only see the tiniest, tiniest hint of the infinite here. History doesn't stretch out behind us. It wraps around us every day like a big coat we wear. We live in the made world of every ancestor, every life before us. Every story as it still unwinds and WHAT, WHAT LADY?"

The whole room kind of gasped all at once and looked around accusingly at people in other rows. People put down their cell phones or picked them up to see if they were ringing or vibrating. People looked to see if their children were behaving. Everyone panicked individually and then closed up like sea anemones. Not me, they all thought. I'm not even here. I didn't come here. Nobody even sees me.

"THIS one, oh, my God. She won't let it go, this one. She's... what are you, a stewardess? She keeps going on about the PLANE—Lady, I don't understand you. I don't know what you're talking about. You make no sense." Micky reached up and grabbed her own forehead in both hands. "She's got this scarf," she flipped one hand gaily over her shoulder like a game show model, "and this CUP of COFFEE. The coffee," Micky lifted her other hand and pretended to hold a dainty cup, her pinky finger extended. "And she's laughing at me, oh, she's got this, this kind of dark, mean laugh."

Coffee cup. Airplane. Uh oh.

"Oh, she thinks this is all so funny. She is so amused at all of us. She's telling me she's not going to let us talk to *anyone.*"

Micky was pacing a little now, in a different gait than her urgent, sweeping moves that had covered the room for the last twenty minutes. Now, she swung her arms ever so slightly. She poised her head between her shoulder blades and turned it as if she were appraising a precious piece of porcelain.

I knew that walk. *Oh, no.*

"Ladies and gentlemen, thank you for coming today. I apologize, but I'm going to have to cut this talk short. Please come again. I do apologize. My website is on the flyers you'll find outside the doors to the conference area. Please contact me for a private reading, and I will do all I can to see that your questions are addressed. Some days just do not go as planned. Thank you for your patience."

I felt incredibly guilty, even though I had no way of knowing what was going to happen. It was my fault. But, I argued to myself, how could I possibly have known Granny would show up? How could that even be true? Why was I even buying into this? She was probably just tired of catering to these demanding people. I had to admit, the details seemed to fit, but you know how it is when you read a horoscope, the stuff that applies you take in, and the excess just rolls off...

"Shut up, woman! Oh my God, she is non-stop. Now she's going on and on about some library. I thought you were a stewardess, now you're a freaking *librarian?*"

The cluster of supplicants still encircling Micky dwindled a bit more at this last outburst. Either she was going to ride this out until every annoyance had been rid, or she actually believed she was talking to somebody. It seemed as though the fifteen or twenty people left were in her personal party of family and friends, along with a couple who had—get this—brought their private detective with them to discuss their daughter's disappearance. Micky had been explaining to them repeatedly that she couldn't find anyone to talk to them, and that, in her experience, meant that odds were good that their daughter was alive. I could tell, whether by supernatural or deductive means I couldn't say, that Micky thought a) the girl was alive, and b) the girl had left on her own and did not want to be found, and c) that these people were doing a whole lot of lying.

I left the security of the window ledge and moved through about half the empty folding chairs so that I could look for an interval. I figured I ought to apologize. It was only right. I'd disrupted the whole show. Meeting. Whatever.

I was trying to compose something in my head that sounded sane right when Micky saw me. She smiled a friendly, professional smile. A random but inevitable one, and genuine, just like when you get a new dental hygienist or vet tech.

"Hi, honey, what can I..."

"I just wanted to apologize," I blurted out, like it was all one word.

Her eyebrows scrunched up a little, so I went on.

"The lady. With the coffee cup. I'm... I think it's..."

"YOU!" Micky pointed at me, and her smile fell, but her face was even friendlier, if that makes sense. I was on a date with a guy one time, and a woman walked up about twenty feet behind him in the restaurant, waved to get my attention and then mouthed "Dump him," while miming a thumbs-down. It was that same face Micky was making now.

"I need to talk to you. Can you come back tomorrow?

I have to go to sleep now. I can't even tell you. But it is imperative that I speak to you. I'm not going to charge you, just, here, take this—can you come at three?" Micky handed me an appointment card. It was a strange-looking appointment card. It had an old globe and pieces of luggage on it.

"I guess I... yeah, yes. Thank you. I'll come tomorrow."

"She's a class-A bitch. I need to talk to you."

"She's a character, yes."

"That's nice of you, honey. She's a bitch. We'll talk tomorrow. Don't worry about today; it happens. They're just like the rest of us. They get angry. They act like children."

So, yeah. I had an appointment with a psychic. I had a little card that told me so.

When I got back the next day I found that she had a booth to herself in the far corner of the display hall, but Micky had a "Keep Calm—Back in a Few" sign up. The same old globe and pieces of luggage from her card—so it wasn't just a travel agency template used randomly. Or figuratively. Maybe it was. But I did feel better about sitting down next to the old leather bags and the friendly figures of North and South America. I traced Hispaniola with one finger and marveled at how far east everything was. My flat-map Mercator projection-deficient worldview was fueled by ancient classroom maps that had only been rolled down in order to cover up the pop quizzes written on the chalkboard. Somehow everything always unraveled a little once I got to the Southern hemisphere.

"Oh, thank goodness you're here. I didn't even write your name down. What's your name, honey?"

"Nicole." Micky shook my hand, then dropped it and hugged me, briefly but tight.

"Your *grandmother*," She tsked.

"I'm really sorry about yesterday. It's not even why I came. To be honest, I don't even remember how I found out—"

"Oh, that—that was not your fault. That's not the first or even the worst time that's happened to me—HA! Don't give it another thought. Sit down, though, because I have to talk to you about this woman. Oh, my. We *have* to talk about this."

She had a lot of cape ends and fringe scarf ends going on, and she seemed to need to sort through them before sitting down. She sat on a low upholstered stool made of a piece of tapestry, maybe an old rug. I sat in the wooden director's chair. It reminded me of one I bought Nora when she was little—she'd carry it into the room, sit it down in front of me and open it ceremoniously if she wanted to talk about something important. I remember watching her run out of the room and come back with the folding chair, setting it down right in front of the TV for the opening number in *Gentlemen Prefer Blondes*. She liked to sing that song with me, "We're just two little girls, from Little Rock."

Micky smiled at me and waited for me to focus.

"Granny was unhappy with me for quite some time, I think."

"Once again, not your fault," she started, and took my hand. "This woman is very angry at a lot of things. She, huhuh, lady, you just—I tell you, she says it's you, that you would not let her go. But she's a selfish one. Don't you let her bully you."

I kind of wanted to defend Granny, but I suspected it wouldn't go well.

"She's one to put everything on somebody else. Nothing is ever her fault. She's her own little island."

Okay. That last part might be true. Yeah, that was pretty true. I never thought about it that way. I just thought it was social anxiety, agoraphobia.

"It's not your job, you know, to defend her." She shook my hand up and down a little, kind of slowly. "You stood by her, you were the only one, and she knows that. I don't think she understands why, even, but you do. And there's these people—I want you to know this, because I want you to know that she's not alone. You are—honey, why are you *so worried* about her? She's gone, you cannot help her over there. But these four people, they can help her if she would listen to them. It's two women and two men. Does that seem right to you? Those people?"

Her husband, and Alice and Willie. Granny and her husband had been married in a double ceremony, and Granny had stayed in touch with Alice her whole life. I never knew what happened in the last year. I couldn't find Alice's address to notify her—I wasn't completely sure she was still alive. After Granny took the overdose of Tylenol PM, not much she said made any sense. I'd always imagined that the two of them clung to each other via their weekly letters until they both started to deteriorate, neither of them noticing that the paper letters were stopping as they each faded, the words and letters dissolving in their watery memories. I couldn't bear thinking of Alice, wherever she might be, wondering what had happened to her friend. But I waited too late to get any location from Granny. *She's my friend,* Granny would say, *don't you remember?*

But who was the other woman? One of her sisters? I wasn't sure.

"By the way, what about the baby? Who's the baby? They're telling me to tell you the baby is with them."

"That's my son." I blurted it out, and Micky nodded.

"That's okay," she said, "They just want you to know, you don't have to tell me anything. They're with him. He's okay. This is all just... Honey, you need to remember, they are much, much more okay than we are. We're still struggling. They are continuous. They are forever. They just love, that's all they do now. Everything is love there."

Tears poured out of my eyes, but no sound. No sobbing or anything. Just came down.

"She needs to go with them. They're waiting for her, and you have to tell her to go. They want me to tell you to tell her—firmly, you have to be firm with her—tell her to leave you and go with them. Oh, she's very angry that I'm telling you this."

"I'm sorry—"

"No. Do not. This is what I do. I'm not afraid of her—" Micky flapped a very jewel-heavy, manicured hand over my right shoulder. "I'm not afraid of you, old lady, and neither is she." Micky seemed like she could have showed up in Narnia with a box of Turkish Delight and kicked the White Queen's ass, and things could have turned out better faster.

"You should stop wearing her jewelry. Just for a while." Micky patted my hand and let it go.

CHAPTER TWELVE

LET'S BE STRAIGHT. I expected things to go wrong. And they did. Just not how I expected.

We bought the property. Looking back, we didn't even discuss it much. One way or another, it seemed like something we had to go through, not around. Everything was okay for a while, mostly. We'd been living out on the OCR—the Old Camden Road—for only a couple of months, in a small prefab house while we worked on plans for a modern, green house, cantilevered over the creek if possible. The planning part was pretty fun, and at the time it made up for having to cross the room sideways and step over the bar stools to get back to the kitchen to get another bowl for morning Rice Krispies.

I woke up early, bouncier than usual, and hungry. I was eating a big bowl of Rice Krispies when Edgar stumbled into the living area in his *Star Wars* pajamas.

"Hey," he mumbled. "Those are my Rice Krispies."

"That's funny. I don't remember you getting your car keys, driving to the Harris Teeter, getting Rice Krispies off the top shelf, taking them to the checkout and paying for a box of Rice Krispies. I don't remember you putting them in a bag and driving home with them. Oh, and then driving back to the store because you forgot the milk."

"Can I have your Rice Krispies?"

"Sure."

When I turned again, I saw two bowls of Rice Krispies on the coffee table. Edgar was perched on his Lego bin as a seat, munching away, until he saw me standing there, dumbfounded.

It's a process, learning the difference between dreams I'm having because I overheard something in a coffee shop or left the TV on *Buying Alaska* all night or because I took too many antihistamines, and the dreams that Actually Really Mean Something. Sadly, most of the dreams that Mean Something do not Mean Something to me. They rarely contain any useful information at all. Although I did recently get a visit from an older gentleman who kind of reminded me of Terence Stamp who informed me that I would remember nothing else of the entire dream, except that when it came time to name the thing that I would need to name, that the name was "Bethel." So indeed, that's all I remember. That's all I got. The guy, I guess I remember him. He was a little impatient with me, like I was pretty stupid. But that it couldn't be helped. He had information he had to give me, and by God I was going to get it and not forget. So I'm holding onto that word, *Bethel*. Sooner or later, I'm going to need to name something. I'm ready.

Last night's dream got me a little stumped, though. It felt like something real, and like a lot of the Mean Something sorts of dreams, I didn't really recognize anybody, and I was pretty sure the body I was in wasn't mine. But I couldn't imagine how watching people building an improvised water slide in a suburban neighborhood had any useful purpose for me. I guess it was just there. Until I maybe one day need it for something.

Or maybe it really is true that stories get lonely and need a place to unfold again. The guy that was there that day—it looked like the late 1970s or early 1980s—maybe he was gone, but this one day, this day he did this really cool thing, that whole story floated around looking for a place to take root. A heart to move to happiness again.

"What you doing, mommy?" Edgar asked, kind of garbled by a mouthful of Krispies.

"Getting a bowl," I started.

"You got a bowl already," said Edgar. He looked up, and I realized he was watching *Teenage Mutant Ninja Turtles*. I didn't remember turning on the TV.

"Let's turn that down. The Turtles are kinda yelling at me. Edgar, are you sitting on the remote?"

Edgar hopped up and held his bowl to the side with both hands, bending all the way around to look behind.

"Nope."

"Well, where'd you put it when you turned on the TV?" Edgar looked up at me, wide-eyed. He kept chewing slowly, but didn't say anything. "Well? Edgar? And you know you're supposed to ask before you turn on the TV."

Now he stopped chewing. Mouth still full, he said, "I didn't turn it on. *You* turned it on. When you were talking on the phone."

"I wasn't talking on the phone. My phone's plugged in by the bed." I wasn't so much arguing with Edgar as trying to unravel what the hell was *happening*. Where was that damn remote? Turtles should not shriek. Or wear headbands. What a world.

"Well, help me find the remote, Edgar. I can't hear myself think."

We both started crawling around on the floor. The whole entire place was less than 800 square feet. This room was probably about 300. The remote wasn't under the sofa, the stairs—not much had an underneath; we had drawers and shelves everywhere to hold all our stuff that wasn't in storage. The time we were spending all jumbled up together had so far been a true adventure, something that drew us up close together. I mean, actually, physically, close. But also it had been a good time. The kids seemed to be digging the daily improvisations. They were less demanding than usual, even. No complaints about space. It wasn't cold anymore, so that helped. We could go outside.

I stood up and looked at the bowl I still had in my hand, half-expecting it to have turned into the remote, because nothing much was looking solid. Edgar slid partway out from under the coffee table and propped his chin up on one hand.

"You get that bowl for the man, mommy?'

"What man? Wait a minute. Just wait. No man. Just a second." I sat down on the sofa and tried to think back over the last—what, ten minutes? Twenty minutes?

Once in a while, it would happen this way. I wouldn't remember until later what the story had been. I couldn't even remember if it was happy or sad or disturbing—I wasn't especially scared, even, until Edgar started talking about the man. But he was also talking to the Ninja Turtles now, and seemed pretty unfazed.

"Is the man friends with the Turtles?" I asked Edgar. I'm not above asking for help, you know.

For the first time all morning, Edgar looked at me like my head was up my behind or something. He sighed a little and shrugged one shoulder, just like his sister.

"Look, I'm just trying to figure out whether or not he needs a bowl of cereal. Or whether he's got the remote, for that matter."

I think the Turtles must have been having an intimate discussion of some kind, being that the pitch seemed to have gone down a notch or two.

"I don't know," Edgar offered, shaking his head slowly. Thomas came down the stairs from the loft.

"Were we making a ruckus? I can't find the remote. Anywhere. How do you lose a freaking remote in this space?"

"Oh, no. I just woke up. Oh, I see. Haha."

"What?"

"You're kidding, right?"

"About which part? I haven't even gotten to the screaming Turtles, the mystery man, the extra bowl of Rice Krispies. Oh, and I've got enough missing time for a brief alien abduction. Check me for probes later, would you?"

Thomas pointed. At first I thought he was pointing at me. But he was pointing to the spot right next to me on the sofa, where the remote sat, plain as the livelong day.

Something was wrong. But what?

Chapter Fourteen

I KEPT MY APPOINTMENT with Micky, despite my reservations about the whole psychic thing. Shit was disappearing. And some of it was important. I finally got around to telling Micky why—or at least why I thought—I had come to her presentation in the first place. Actually, once I started talking about it, I got kind of jumbled up and confused. Yes, I read about her work with archaeologists. But I can't remember how or why. I clicked on a link in the article about her to get to the Head, Heart and Spirit Convention webpage, but how had I found the article? Especially since there didn't seem to be any such article when later I went to find it.

"It doesn't matter," Micky said, "you found your way here. That's what's important. We find what we need, when we need it."

She had pretty much the same thing to say about my rickety understanding of what may or may not be the supernatural parade of narratives marching through my daily consciousness.

"It seems like it ought to be, you know, useful," I said to her, looking around to see if anyone might recognize me here. Or not recognize me and call a big 'shenanigans' on this whole conversation.

"Well, if you decide it's something you want to work on, that part will become obvious. You'll know."

"So, is there any way to... practice... or at least mediate..."

"Right now you need to focus on your boundaries. You walk into a room and it knocks the wind out of you, all the emotions, all this stuff that isn't yours but you take it on. Your first job is to find the part that's you and keep it separate. You can't take all of it into yourself, or you'll lose what's you, and you'll have a big angry mess. All the anger and fear will drown out everything else. But listen, it doesn't have to be that way. You know what's happening. Just practice reminding yourself, this is not my emotion. This belonged to somebody else. You ever balance your chakras? You can start there. Whatever you believe, a good, methodical meditation won't hurt and could certainly help."

I remembered something vague about chakras from my LA days.

"So, should I get a book…"

"Get a tape or a—what do you call it—you have one of those iPod things? My kids got me one. You can download them from anywhere." She leaned in confidentially and glanced over her shoulder and mine. "Don't buy anything from these people here. I guess you know this already, but most of these people are completely insane. It's a freak show."

Micky disappeared like a donkey with a broom tied to its tail, erasing all traces. Her website is gone—hell, it was never really there; just a merchant template that was never filled in. The phone number on the business card is disconnected.

I'd like to think she was a real person. But if that's not true, and I did imagine it, I have to give my subconscious some credit for a damn good show.

Either way, I'd have liked to have run into her again, because I had all kinds of exciting stuff to tell her about what happened when I downloaded my chakra-balancing podcast. Plus, there was the chat I had with Granny.

I started last year with two sets of human remains. I'm only in half as much trouble now, on that score at least. I figured leaving Granny's ashes at the library-in-progress had to have reduced my debt to the spirit world. I still have my son's ashes, and I've been spending more time trying to open my mind to whatever clues the universe is willing to give me about that resolution. So far, the universe had been conspicuously silent. Deepening my belief that when bad things happen to children, there is no meaning to be derived except that there are just no guarantees in this world and that some experiences don't teach you anything. So far the universe's answers regarding my son's death ran along the same lines as the responses of strangers: "Oooh." "Oh, that's terrible." "I am so sorry." By the way, these are all appropriate answers. Thoroughly appropriate. Also appropriate is the quick distraction or exit. Believe me, it's what I'd do, given the circumstances, if I could. The universe has pretty much just looked at me with a bewildered expression and then suddenly had to take a phone call.

I'm still not sure what Granny's thoughts are on having her ashes interred under the new county library, but there haven't been any mysterious fires or dining room chairs flying through the house. Nobody has been hearing voices in the TV. I guess what I learned from the whole thing—and you were probably waiting for me to figure this part out—is that those ashes were still part of this physical world, and so they matter more to those of us still in the physical world than they do to our folks on the other side. They only care inasmuch as that stuff bothers us.

In the meantime, I downloaded a podcast to help balance my chakras. Lord have mercy. It wasn't too bad, really. The lady had this childlike voice and charming Australian accent. I had it on my iPod for weeks and couldn't find time to listen to it because it took like twenty freaking minutes to balance your chakras. I was an impatient American consumer. I wanted the instant chakra-balancing tool. Couldn't I just step into a tube every morning that would balance my chakras and tell me I don't have cancer? Let's work on that. I thought we should have had that before Viagra.

I had the iPod on Shuffle one afternoon, so it came up randomly, the chakra-balancing podcast. I knew it was a seriously bad judgment moment for me, but I was stuck in traffic, bored, curious, nervous.

"Lie down on your back and close your eyes."

I'd skip that part, for obvious reasons.

"Find a neutral mind space. It can be any space that works for you. Free your mind from judgment."

Check. Yes. Judgment-free.

"For this next set, we will begin to open your chakras, one by one. Now, it will be important, once we finish, that you also return to each point and close each chakra according to the process. You do not want to re-enter the world with your chakras open, because then you will be absorbing all kinds of energies and it will be very difficult to protect yourself."

So, you're saying to yourself, here is the point in the recording where you turn it off, because you're in traffic and all. That's what a decent person would do. Or at least a person as risk-averse as I typically am. I won't make a phone call if it's 13 minutes past the hour. Yes, really. I never jaywalk. Ever. I have a mental ritual when I pass a cemetery, but, as will come as no surprise to you, that ritual is ridiculously elaborate and so personal as to make less than zero sense to anybody else.

"Your root chakra is at the base of your spine, and it is associated with the color red."

I was only thinking about what a red lotus would look like, what a lotus root would look like, about the Lotus-Eaters and whether they ate red lotuses, whether "lotuses" is the plural of "lotus," and about that Ellen Voigt poem that had to do with floating lotuses. Or maybe lilies. Something about wrestling with them. They don't have roots exactly, do they? Because they float.

I was in my car, in a state of near bliss. And then the car behind me hit me. I wasn't moving. It wasn't my fault. The officer said so. All the same, I'm pretty glad my root chakra wasn't all the way open or anything, because I'm not sure how that would have turned out or how the emergency room conversation would have gone. As it was, it was all very minor and no mention of chakras had to come up at all, until I got home.

"So tell me again what you were doing when the car hit you?" Thomas sat down. When I got to the end of our new road, he had been out on the property, pacing off the measurements for the cellar out where they'd be coming to dig the foundation in a week or so. But when he yelled over to me, "How was the rest of your day?" I yelled back, "Fine! I only got hit a little bit by a car." Then he yelled, "WHAT?" and I waved and called out, "I got a bit HIT by a LITTLE CAR," and I walked away toward our tiny temporary house, up the hill, while he stood with both hands raised over his head, his arms in a big Y shape, and I briefly yelled back over my shoulder, "NOT A BIG CAR IT'S ALL FINE."

The night before, we had cooked a bunch of stuff on the grill, some steaks for that night and some sausage the farmer from down the road had given us. I planned on making some marinara and sweet peppers to go with the sausage, and I had already dropped the garlic and oil into the pan to heat and was getting some rolls out of the freezer by the time Thomas made it through the door.

"Call me crazy," he began, and I glanced up to smile, a fake smile, but we have a deal about fake smiles so I don't feel guilty. "...but it sounded like you said you got hit by a car."

"First of all, my car got hit by a car, not me." Thomas's arms were still making a Y shape, but this time his hands were pointed down, palms up.

"There's not much damage. Just a scrape."

"Are you still talking about the car?"

"Oh heavens yes. I'm not a bit damaged. My root chakra was not open."

He's pretty great at rolling with stuff. But he was still a *husband*, you know. So I got one of those looks. Because that's his job. Other women get them all the time. Me, not so much. But they still count.

So once he sat down, I explained about the lady with the Australian accent and about the lotuses and everything. Thomas didn't know what the correct plural of "lotus" was, either, and he didn't seem to want to talk about it much. I did agree to take the podcast off my iPod. I figured it wasn't going to work all that well if I couldn't lie down and close my eyes.

"Have you tried it yet? I mean, besides in traffic?"

"To be fair, we were stopped."

"Was the car on? I can't believe it. Are you the same person who will not answer a cell phone in the car—"

"Okay, okay. No, I guess today was about as much as I've listened to it. It's twenty minutes long—I don't have twenty minutes to lie down on the floor."

The garlic was starting to burn. I reached over and shook the pan hard, cut down the heat. Thomas came over and turned the burner all the way off.

"Go right now. I'll take the kids to Bojangles."

"But I've got dinner started. We already made sausages, and the sauce is started..."

"We'll eat the sausages tomorrow. Go. Align those things. Whatever they are."

"Well. I guess I could give it a shot."

"What's the worst case? You get a twenty minute nap?"

It was hard to argue with a worst-case scenario that included a nap.

"Okay. Bring me back some of that chow chow."

"They call it slaw."

"Fine. And some tea."

"You don't want any chicken?"

I thought about it. I hate chickens. I can't even bring

myself to eat them, normally, because I hate them so much and I don't want to take in even a single bite of their evil, brutal stupidity. Once in a while, I will eat some chicken tenders from Bojangles. I feel terrible for days afterwards. I feel mean and stupid and half-plucked.

"No thanks. Just the slaw and the tea."

It took me a good fifteen minutes to find a pair of headphones, rifling through piles of beautifully designed Apple detritus scattered everywhere: mine, Thomas's, Nora's. Even Edgar has an iPad now. We are all so plugged in. I worry about it every day. When I get that far on my to-do list: number seventeen, "Fear abstraction." Like all southerners, I worry about it. But on the arc of existential detachment, it seems like we know a lot of other people who are a lot farther out from shore than we are. I know it doesn't really matter what other people are doing. I know I am happiest when I don't have a TV. But I also know that when I met people in grad school who said things like, "Oh, I grew up with no TV," if they were neo-hippie, they usually struck me as pretty insincere and annoying. It also seemed like if you just spontaneously started singing the theme from *Good Times* or *Facts of Life,* they miraculously jumped right in, knew all the words and everything. Now, I know people who grew up with only sporadic TV because their dad would hock it, when he was around, and they'd have to go to their cousins' trailer to watch *Battle of the Network Stars* or *James at 15.* Those people love TV. It has a value for them. Some of my only happy memories of my father are of watching *The Gong Show.* Him jumping off the couch and dancing like Gene, Gene the Dancing Machine.

Everything is complicated. Everything has these intrica-cies. That's true all over America, but in the South, there's more layers and they all have names. Some have two names. You know. Like Billie Joe or Bobbie Jean.

I finally got the headphones untangled and plugged into the laptop. I lined up part one of the podcast and sat down at the coffee table in front of the screen. I used to lie down on the floor of my room and hold the album cover over my head to listen to music. Now I stare at this screen, this long list.

Almost immediately I realize the problem: she's already telling me to lie down and close my eyes, the earphone cord won't allow me to lie down on the floor and I can't get flat on the sofa, and in a few minutes she's already going on again about my root chakra while I'm hopping around the coffee table on one foot with one eye closed balancing the laptop on one hand and carrying a cushion from the couch in the other.

I have a problem relaxing. It's the plain truth. Thomas evacuated the house tonight as a way of telling me he could see it, my avoidance of any kind of meditative experience, even if my planning, list-checking side wanted to use the remedy I'd potentially found for my problem. I just didn't want to *have* to do it. What if something weird happened, if I had some creepy encounter or something? I'm really too timid to do much of anything on purpose. If not for the pleasant but extremely vigorous contact high I encountered in a friend's dorm room in college, I'd have never had any drug experiences at all. After insisting there was Absolutely Nothing Happening when accused of being stoned off my gourd, my friend's dealer pointed out that I might be Fine and Good but I'd been trying to turn off the same lamp for twenty minutes, twisting the knob the wrong direction and giving a little peep every time it clicked but stayed on.

After having to get up one last time to get a blanket, since the floor turned out to be chillier than I thought I could stand for twenty whole minutes, I backtracked to the beginning of the podcast. Or at least back to where it started in earnest.

I'm not sure I'm ever going to be able to remember what happens in this podcast. I'd recommend it, if you're a squirrelly sort like myself, but I'm not sure yet what the long-term effects are going to be. Something happened, but I usually remember what happens in my head better than what that lady is saying. And I learned my lesson about listening to it anyplace but when I'm on the floor. I followed all her directions pretty explicitly. Didn't want to be walking around with my chakras hanging out.

So that first time, the Bojangles night, I went through the root chakra, moving up the spine, everything going just great but fairly unremarkable, until we got to the green one. That's when I started to feel like stuff was going on around me, and that I had to be vigilant and keep my eyes closed. By the time we got to the top of my head, I forget what you call it, she started talking about the kind of light you might see and the ways it might manifest, I was so far into my head that I only remember the part where she got to what I was seeing, I thought, *that's it,* and I guess I stopped listening.

Because a milky, translucent figure was standing next to me. A lightbulb man, that's how I think of him. His head was shaped a little like a lightbulb, not the squiggly ones, but the ones like you'd use on an old fashioned strand of outdoor Christmas lights. And he was lit up like that, like a glow inside him that spread through his body in veins like electrical wiring. *This is how they got the electricity here from the Poodle Planet,* I thought, remembering Nora's cosmology. He bent his lightbulb head down and squared it with mine as I lay there on the floor, in my tiny house sitting on the spot where, growing up, I used to pretend I had built my own town, cooking dandelions and wild onions in my toy pots and pans. The place where I dug up arrowheads and quartz pieces as big as my hand. He squared his face—but he had no face—above mine, and then he reached right over my head and grabbed something with the end of his arm made of light. He stood up and he flung it. He turned and he flung whatever it was toward the window, and he watched it, as if he wanted to make sure it was gone.

He stayed with me for a while. Maybe he thought it would come back. Even now I don't know what it was, and I don't know if I would recognize it if it returned. Maybe he knows. Sometimes I think about that light, and I feel protected—even if that's silly. I have a medal of St. Michael from New Orleans, a little painted oval. I wear it because it makes me feel the same way. Superstition. Compulsive disorder. Sleeping on the side of the bed away from the doorway or the window. Not stepping on cracks. Knocking on wood. Don't talk to me about ladders. The world is littered with hazards we don't even think about. Our avoidance of them is hardwired in. No book should have a chapter 13.

CHAPTER FIFTEEN

FINGERS. THEY WERE MINE. I was pretty sure. I closed and
opened them, closed and opened. A dog down the road
was barking, but Toast just shifted in her sleep. Part of the
meditation, coming back to reality, has you open and close
your hands, feeling the fingers. Five sisters. Five sisters.

That's right, I thought. My father's mother and his four
aunts. My mother's mother and her four aunts. Five sisters
on each side, holding me up.

If only they could get me out of bed. Either my aunts
or my fingers, I don't care which. I could hear the coffee
maker going—since we'd moved to the woods, Thomas
often sets it the night before. It is so quiet out here and
so cozy with all of us asleep in the tiny house, the kids up
in the loft. Going back into town every day keeps getting
harder.

I could hear Nora clunking down the loft stairs, so
I managed to clamber out of bed and meet her in the
kitchen.

"I had a dream about rodents." She put her head down
on the kitchen counter and let out a slow whine.

"Ugh. Nightmare?"

"No, nice rodents. Big ones, like capybaras. They were
wearing hats." She stood, took a deep breath, and flapped
the blanket she was wearing like a cape.

"Oh, well. I dreamed I got two new tattoos, a Sphinx
head and a Masonic third eye, on the backs of my thighs."

Nora peered over the rim of the coffee cup she had
overfilled and was carefully slurping.

"Mom, did you join the Illuminati?"

I thought about it. Not for effect or anything; I was really thinking. Not whether I'd joined of course, but whether I could think of anything funny to say about the Illuminati.

"I can't remember." That was all I had.

"So, then, 'yes.'" Nora smiled and poured more peppermint creamer, hoarded from her Christmas supply, into her oversized cup. She can usually get the peppermint creamer to last past Easter.

"Anyway. What on earth would the Illuminati want with me?"

"That," she said, tipping the cup to drain it, "is exactly how they get in. Want to go take some pictures with me tonight?"

"Tonight? Where?"

"I heard there's this old orphanage behind where the TV station is—"

"Oh no, come on. You've been suckered with these urban legends, haven't you? That place is haunted, yes, and not in a horror movie way, just a sad, pitiful, rot-your-soul—"

"Hey, if you're scared—"

"THAT will not work on me. I really don't get the sense that it's scary—seriously, if you're going for that, there are scarier places. Why don't you go hang out in Oakwood like we used to?"

Oakwood is our oldest municipal cemetery. Officially, I guess. Because, you understand, in the South, it used to be that certain kinds of people could only be buried in certain kinds of places, and some of those places don't have names or markers or anything. Oakwood is pretty old. I wonder if there any trailer parks, apartment complexes or subdivisions or communities of any kind, or at least of any kind that includes living people, named Oakwood. I think I'll look that up later.

"Oakwood's not scary."

"You're not listening right, then."

"Well, so if it's no big deal, just come with us."

"Who's going?"

"Me and D and K."

"Why are all your friends letters? You're like secret spy kids. Teens in Black." They were in black, actually. I just thought they were Goths, but hey. I reminded myself not to look into any of their flashlights.

"Uh huh. We're watching you for the Illuminati. They've invested a lot of time."

"Okay, so if it's not supposed to be scary, why do we have to go at night?"

"Because. Flash photography. That's the whole point; I'm practicing."

"So many things you could take pictures of in the dark."

"You've seen it; why can't we see it?"

"We used to drive by it almost every day—get them to come out here; it's plenty dark out here."

"Hm. Maybe later. When you get your goats."

I'd been threatening to raise fainting goats on the

property, but I was waiting until we got a little settled in. I felt a deep affinity with fainting goats that, frankly, shouldn't be that hard to understand.

"Don't tie this nonsense to my hypothetical goats."

"Just come and stop arguing. You know you're going to come anyway."

I did know, in fact, that I was going along. I had known it from the beginning of the conversation. I know that I knew because I had already secretly decided what I was going to wear and was now thinking about where the last place I had seen my tripod might have been. I was pretty sure Edgar was using it as a light saber a few days back.

I let Nora drive since she knew where the rest of the alphabet lived. I sat in the back of the car clutching my tripod and wearing Thomas's old trench coat with the deep pockets. Once the vehicle filled up, the conversation sounded like a cross between a Sesame Street short film and a scene out of Tarantino.

"K, did you bring a crowbar, just in case we have to get in through a window?"

"This is a terrible plan."

"No, we won't need one. J got in a couple of nights ago."

"This is such a terrible plan."

"Mom, *don't* make me regret inviting you." Frosty-toned little thing. I don't know where she gets this attitude from.

"If I'm to be part of this donnybrook, I insist on being referred to as M."

"Well. That's going to be confusing."

"Is that letter taken by one of your cohorts already?
Then I'll be Q."

"No chance that's going to stand for 'quiet,' is there?"

"Nope. No more than your N standing for 'nice.'"

"Well then. Here we are."

Amateurs. The whole backstory for this ridiculous location
had been woven into 1980s teenage local horror culture. A
former girl scout myself, this adventure struck me as watery
and pathetic. But creepy people had been known to hang
out around here, looking for some kind of excitement. So
I didn't want my creepy little troop to go there alone. And
clearly they were going. I went and *my* parents didn't have
any idea, so at least there was that.

"Where is it that y'all think you are, exactly?"

"Crybaby Lane! This is it. Everybody out; soon we'll
be hearing the wailing of the tortured souls." I believe
it was the Agent K person making this pronouncement.
It was dark in the back seat, and we had parked next to a
massive wall of underbrush. Possibly the only underbrush
left in the vicinity after all the construction on NC State's
Centennial Campus in the last ten years.

"What are you talking about?" I really was baffled; we
were not at the location I expected. Urban legends get
screwed up so fast.

"The orphans in the tragic fire..." K made rainbow
motions with her arms and spoke in a husky drawl.

"You all do watch too much TLC. You sound like a bad
voiceover." Nora had grabbed her camera bag, but she
stood outside the car with the driver door open, halfway
committed.

"For a generation with so much random information available to you, you seem particularly incapable of research. Crybaby Lane. Where on earth did you get your directions from?"

"That's Bilyeu Street, and if we walk down this lane, we'll smell the smoke from the tragic fire that killed all those orphans..." D seemed to be working from some ragged piece of handwritten notes.

"The only smoke you'll smell down that lane is from crack pipes. We're not going over there. You people. Can't even scare yourselves right. Get in the car."

"No, this is it! This is where the orphanage was. Right here! Look, on the map—"

"I don't know whose crappy, hand-drawn, not-to-any-scale map this is, but look around—all of this land was orphanage at one time or another. The church owned acres and acres. It was a Catholic community called Nazareth. Gah. Read a website once in a while, why don't you."

"Well, there's not much to photograph here. Unless I'm doing studies of Red Bull cans and condom wrappers." Nora balanced on one foot and squinted. It was unclear why.

"But. I want to hear the babies," K fake-sulked.

"Okay. First of all, ew. Second, if what you want is to be scared, get in the CAR. I can show you where to get scared."

I'd have never gone there on my own. I was just as risk-averse as a teenager as I am as an adult. Now, if I got really mad or really righteous about something, then I'd be fearless to the point of careless. So that's sort of how it all happened.

My Crybaby Lane story started when I was about their age, and it wasn't one I had told many times. But it was one I remembered all these years, and don't think I didn't consider it a few times when we moved within a mile of the place. For somebody who used to have to lie down on the floor of an apartment bedroom before I'd lease it—I'd have to know I could sleep in the room—I did have a moment when I thought about whether or not I could live near the old Cardinal Gibbons High School. That's what was standing near the old orphanage back when I was in high school.

It was the night of the Cardinal Gibbons' High School Dance. Gibbons was the private Catholic high school in town. I was Catholic myself, but *nobody* from my country parish went to Gibbons. Gibbons was full of rich kids, transplants from up North whose dads and moms worked for IBM or Burroughs Wellcome out in the Research Triangle Park. They lived in North Raleigh, in the subdivisions all named for the things that weren't actually there anymore: Black Horse Run. Walden Woods. Possum Track Road.

My dad's restaurant catered the dance. He'd been doing a big business at the time with the transplant community. He spoke fluent Yankee, being half-Yankee on his father's side. He at least knew how to pretend that yes, he could cater a Kosher bat mitzvah. He'd throw everything in a Hebrew Nationals box and just roll.

Somehow my dad got my high school boyfriend and me to help him load in and out. Since it was my dad, I'm sure it was some kind of hustle and no cash, but there we were. So after the dance started, we wound up with a couple of hours to kill. We ran into this skinny red-headed kid—I can't remember his name—who came to the punk rock shows. After a bit of awkwardness at recognizing each other, the three of us ended up behind the gymnasium smoking cigarettes and discussing how weird it was that he went to a Catholic high school when I was the Catholic one.

"My dad says the public schools down here have science textbooks that say we haven't landed on the moon yet."

I said it sounded like his dad was living in outer space himself.

"Hey, you know there's an old orphanage at the end of that path over there. Just what's left of it after it burned."

"Oh yeah?" I couldn't tell if my boyfriend was being polite or was genuinely interested. The kid was showing off, though, so it didn't matter. We all knew what was going to happen.

I got angrier and angrier while we were tromping up the hill.

"Hey, hey," the kid stopped, "Can you smell that? They say that smoky sweet smell is from the burning flesh."

"That smoky sweet smell is from your stupid clove cigarettes, you idiot. You know, this is completely wrong. Who even told you about this place?"

"Man, the nuns and the priests all know about it at my school."

"So they told you?"

"No, they won't talk to us about it. But they all know."

"And you're all just a bunch of genius mind readers yourselves. This is stupid. There's nothing—"

And I stopped on the path. There was a man following us, just off the path, in the high grass. I started walking again and I tried whispering over to my boyfriend, *there's somebody over there,* but the red-headed kid kept going on about the orphanage fire.

"Yeah, it was like in the 1950s and somebody turned over a kerosene lamp, and the whole place blew up in flames."

"Okay, first of all, people didn't still use kerosene lamps in the fifties. Not like as a normal thing. So this is just some stupid bullshit seventh grade ghost story."

"No, they were poor orphans! They probably had to use like the old technology and stuff."

"Kind of like your dad's brain."

I heard it again, and I almost could see him. This whole idea—what had I been thinking? I hated these stupid catering jobs. My dad was always pulling something jacked up, lying about something, breaking stuff, charging people too much. Now because I got suckered into this—and all because he let me bring my boyfriend; we weren't even getting paid—now I was going to get killed by a vagrant in a stupid field.

I kept walking, kept pace with the boys, stayed in the middle of the path. The figure was just slightly behind us to the right, keeping pace, too.

Finally the kid stopped. "Do you hear that?" he said.

Before I knew what I was doing, I wheeled around and punched him, right square in the nose. He was totally innocent, unsuspecting, and a little blood trickled from his left nostril. I was short and small, but I was really pissed, and he was clueless.

"WHAT the fuck!"

"That's IT!" I shouted, balling up my fist and squaring up again. "You tell your friend to come out of the goddam bushes, or I swear, I will hit you again!"

My boyfriend was squatting there with his arms spread out like he was tracking a pop fly. "Nicole, what the—? What are you doing?"

"He's set us up, don't you see? He's trying to scare us—some dude's been following us since we left the gym—I tried to tell you, but he won't shut up long enough to—"

"I swear I didn't—"

"I WILL HIT YOU again," I said, pointing at the kid, "SHUT IT." I turned back to my boyfriend. "This asshole," I said, "thinks we are stupid. You little Yankee shit," I said, turning back to the kid. "You and your dad can take your super-NASA smart asses back to New Jersey. If it's so great up there, how come you assholes keep moving down here and buying up all the farms and getting rid of the cows and the food and building your ugly fake cotton planter houses—by the way, this is not WILLIAMS-BURG, genius! This is NORTH CAROLINA! What is WRONG with all of you?"

Now both of them were staring at me like I was insane.

"Tell your friend to come out. Now. Or I swear, I will beat you both to death with my shoe, and teenage kids will be coming out here in twenty years to hear your fucking screams, you douche."

I thought he might cry. "I don't! There's nobody! I SWEAR!"

I stood there for a second. He wasn't lying. I always knew when people were lying. I knew that even back then. He was more scared than I was. For a few more seconds at least.

I felt him, over there in the grass, watching us. *Don't,* he was saying. *Don't go up there.* He just stayed there, hidden. Something was wrong. He was hurt. *It's dangerous. Let me save you. I can save you. You've got to get out of here.*

"We've got to go." I said.

"Wait, but—"

"RUN!" I yelled and I shoved my boyfriend ahead of me back down the path, toward the gymnasium where I could still hear the strains of "Panama" blasting out of the cracked-open windows.

The teenagers, then and now, were *right* about Crybaby Lane. But like it often seems to be, people know when something's, you know, off, but we tend to attach our own narratives to the feeling that's familiar. The land around what the cool kids call Crybaby Lane holds a lot of pain. That's why people made up such an awful story about an orphanage fire to explain what they felt when they walked down that dark road. But the real story's just as sad.

These girls don't know that only a few months ago, I read about the selling off of the church's property. One day soon after, I pulled over and walked down to the greenway path, looking for the ridge where that night, in the tall grass behind the gym full of rich kids dancing to Van Halen, I met a sad, lost spirit. Scared the shit out of us, no lie. But he didn't mean to.

I couldn't really find it, the path from the Gibbons gym. With so many buildings gone, all the underbrush removed, everything mowed down—about the only thing I could recognize was the enormous tree that stood at the entrance to the diocese offices, a building that continued to house orphans until the mid-1970s. It would have been about ten years after they turned it from orphanage to offices that I spent my strange evening here.

Nothing—all quiet. It was a Tuesday afternoon, not much traffic. Just before people would be coming home from work. He was gone. Maybe for good. Nothing looked familiar to me, so probably not to him, either.

I just wanted to know who he was. Maybe he did save us from something, back then. This part of town was a lot more dangerous then. Heck, that's why the Transplants moved the school not long after. Southwest Raleigh was in decline in those days. It hit bottom somewhere in the nineties, like many of us. Now it was bouncing its way back up again.

Walking back up Nazareth Street, I knew I needed to find out who he was.

See, if I'd been born in this whole age of the Internet, the democratization of information, maybe I'd have never doubted any of my visitations. It would have been a whole lot easier to track some thread of truth in them. It was pretty simple, because the lies are recorded as scrupulously as the facts are, so once you start digging, you're pretty sure to figure out not only what you need but where everybody else has gone wrong.

So, here's the scoop on the legend and the reality, because I looked it all up, and here's what I read. Cross-

referenced and everything. The whole orphanage fire
tragedy came logically enough into being as a local
legend, since there were a few actual fires. Just none
quite as dramatic as the Crybaby Lane Orphan Killer.
Fires happened, particularly in the nineteenth and early
twentieth centuries. These had all been fairly mundane in
source, one in 1961 that seemed to be mostly misadventure
relating to a wasp eradication project gone bad. Confined
to a nonresidential area, it was a source of embarrassment
for the priests who had set the nests off in the first place,
then somehow weren't prepared for the sudden breeze
that whipped up the balls of angry insects into torches that
quickly burned the rectory to the ground. And then what
must have been a terrifying blaze at the stables, in the 1910s
or thereabouts. Not much information, but it did look like
some horses had been lost. That would have been a mess.

I kept reading, beginning to think I'd have to rely once
again on my own nerves that found this character. And
then there he was. Not in the orphanage at all, but the
seminary, and that made sense. He didn't know why we
were there on the path.

He was there on the path because when the fire started,
he made it all the way outside. But he went back in to get
the others. He was strong. And angry—it was a stupid fire;
why was it happening? And nobody followed the plans, the
plans—you weren't supposed to leave people on your hall,
that's not what we do! He ran back in, snatching open every
door. All the way to the top, he led them.

They were boys, on the upper floors, boys who were
studying to be priests. Teenagers from the orphanage.

He tried to get them down the stairs but the smoke was
thicker below. They went to the roof.

You've got to jump!

Some of them were crying. They huddled back away from the ledge. The roof was hot already, and any second the flames would break, and they'd all drop down into the inferno.

Listen! He yells at them. *You don't have any choice! It's the only way! You'll die if you don't! Don't you understand?*

He took one of the smallest ones, lifted him up and tossed him to the men standing below. Then another. They panicked, started to run away from him. The scrawny one, the redhead, he jumped on his own. But the big one, the baby. He grabbed his arm and pulled him toward the edge of the building.

We've got to go! Now! But he was blubbering, he cried every night, this one. His mother had abandoned him and he never got over it, waited at the window for her every afternoon until he was fifteen and they sent him to the seminary, still sobbing, her picture worn to leather from the years of his tears, her face a blur. He couldn't bear the thought of him dying on this roof, the pointlessness, the frivolousness of the woman who had left him, how she walked back down the steps to the waiting carriage. She'd worn no gloves, but the carriage was decent. What was wrong with her? Had that even been his mother? Grandmother? The boy had no chance, born to careless people, what kind of world puts people like that in charge of children? What kind of God? John was his name. He called the boy John, too, this boy left by the woman with no gloves and no sense. He would not see him die on this roof, in this pointless fire.

He punched him, hard. It wasn't the first time in his life he'd struck a man, and he knew how to knock him out.

He'd land easy that way; he waved over the men holding the sheet and they stretched it out, and he let the boy go like a bird from the nest.

The priests were confused. They thought he'd been hurt in the fall, and they clustered around trying to rouse him as the flames were coming up behind John, the last man left on the roof. He waved and yelled for them to pick up the sheet, but they seemed to have forgotten him for a second, and he didn't even have the second to give. He jumped, knowing it was only the manner of pointless death he was choosing.

"I am your servant!" he called out as he fell. His heart broken, knotted entirely with pain, he thought, *I am your servant, but you have chosen not to use me.*

Chapter Sixteen

I rolled the car up onto the dead grass at a flat part in the curb. I parked, but I left the headlights burning for a minute. I waited to see if I could feel him. Finally I shut off the lights and turned to the teenaged super-spies, who had gotten a little more interested and serious once I said I was tired of their nonsense and that from here on, I'd be doing the driving.

"So. We've now arrived at the scene of a horrible, detestable, despicable crime of such cruelty its name can hardly be spoken in the civilized world. I myself was a witness to the calamity. It was... it was..."

I looked away for a moment, then turned back suddenly, my flashlight drawn up to illuminate my face from the chin up.

"...it was *a high school dance!*"

They all screamed with delight and we piled out of the car.

"So, a field. Wow. Super scary." Nora paced around. I could feel her circling about fifty feet away. We could spread out but still see each other completely, because the last building had been torn down and the property leveled about four years ago. Cardinal Gibbons had been shut, dismantled and rebuilt farther out of town in a place that looked even more generic and appealing to the Transplants.

"See that tree over there in the middle? That was where the driveway circle was. The tree was by the entrance."

"Oh look! You can see there's still a path here. K, come over here!"

A bright flash startled me, but it was just Nora, testing. She saw me jump.

"Ha. Sorry." She pointed to her camera. "Maybe if I set the tripod up on that ridge over there, I can get a time-lapse shot of the car headlights down there on Western."

"Yeah. I think that could work. It might look cool because it would be kind of intermittent—"

One of the Alphabet Squad was shrieking, crouched in the dark past the big tree, almost to the side street that bordered one edge of the property. We started jogging over to her.

"It's a *grave!*" she wailed. There was no way to tell whether this discovery excited or horrified her.

"Oh, hang on," I called over, and then I said to Nora "...there's almost no way that's what it is, but let's see."

"It's got birth and death dates!" D has a shriek that could pierce a can of tuna.

"Well? So does a Wikipedia article," Nora chirped, taking a picture of the marker, and the flash startled me again for a second. When my eyes adjusted, the girls were clustered around the camera screen.

"It in no way says she's buried here. But yeah, it's a little creepy." Nora looked at K and D on either side of her to see if they were going to argue the point. They just kept staring at the screen.

"It's worth noting here," I started, "that this was only one of the buildings used as an orphanage around here. Like I said before, this whole place used to be a Catholic community."

"Well, where's the one that burned down?" K looked around in the dark.

"There were like three different fires. See, this is the thing about these urban legends. People get excited, and the ghoulishness just gets piled on—" I gestured around, waving about at all corners of the field, but the girls were impatient.

"*Three* fires? Were they *trying* to kill all the orphans?" D looked up and squinted—lit by the camera screen, they all looked about ten years old, huddled around a campfire. *That's what I could see: little girls around a fire. I felt a surge of safety and happiness, excitement. Like I did at camp, up late in the night, but instead of being alone in my insomnia, surrounded by other little girls. Drowsy and safe. I could feel my cheeks getting warm. I touched them; they were round from smiling and warm from the fire. I hadn't been warm in so long. The girls had cups of popcorn, metal cans they held over the flame until the kernels popped up. Laughing every time the pop happened. Sometimes a spark would flash, and I could see their faces in the light...*

K was asking me a question. I tried to re-focus.

"No, listen—nobody died in any of those fires. Well, mostly." I was about to explain the man in the tall grass to them, but I paused, trying to figure out how to avoid the part about needlessly punching a skinny red-haired boy.

"Except *her*," they turned the camera around so that I could see the display screen. "*She* died in the fire. One of those fires."

"Let me see this. Wait, I don't want to see it." I stepped back and held my hand in front of my face, like I was blocking another flash from the camera. Right here on the screen. It was going to tell me something I didn't want to know.

"How old was she?" I asked the girls, my hand still over my eyes. It was quiet for a few seconds, then I heard Nora's voice.

"She was seven. Wouldn't have had her birthday yet that year."

"Okay." I said. "Okay. I'm okay. Sorry." I sat down on the ground and put out my flashlight for a minute. I kept feeling my cheeks. They felt like they were on fire.

"What happened to her?" When I looked up, they were all standing around me.

"I told you this was sad, not scary." Now I was having trouble getting the shake out of my voice.

"Okay, Mom, we feel terrible enough. What happened to her?"

"How should I know? You're the ones that found the marker. That's more information than I've got."

I wondered how this all felt to them. For so long, I couldn't imagine that other people didn't see and feel the same things I did. It would be as if people were walking on this plot of land with us going, "*What* tree? *What* marker? I don't see any cars or moon or faint traces of paths, the paths the orphans would use when they walked down to the train station to go to their summer camp at the coast, the one the nuns would march the cows down, because the cows still had to be milked and had to be taken on the train with the students... I don't see any of those things that are here."

"Did any of you feel... warm? Or kind of... happy and safe?" Maybe one of them noticed the same things.

"Um, there are a lot of things I expected you to ask us,

but that wasn't at the top of the list," said K.

"That's how it goes, though—" Funny, I thought, I'm not sure anybody other than Thomas has ever had the chance to see it this clearly. "That's exactly how it goes. I felt warm, happy, sleepy—I felt like I was with this group of people like me, and they were watching over me. And that's it. Like we were sitting right here around a campfire in the dark, but that everything was completely fine."

The girls all looked around. "Well? Maybe she's lonely. And now we're here."

It's a good thing the Alphabets couldn't see me ugly-crying in the dark, how the tears, silently and profusely, started coming. I couldn't stop. That's it. Somehow, the light, the girls. Those things reminded her, the little one, the name on the marker—we reminded her of her happiest time. Right before it happened. It was the first really cold night of the year, and they went out to where the trash fires were burning. When she got too close, her blanket, her wraps caught a spark. They all called out to her to stop, but she couldn't stop running. If she could have stopped running. But she couldn't. She knew the girls were trying to save her. They had protected her and kept her safe since she came to that place. She loved them, her beautiful friends, the big girls that combed her hair and hugged her when she woke up crying. They were calling out to her. But she was running, so fast, as long as she could run fast it didn't hurt, and soon she was running toward it, not away from them, no, no, she couldn't ever really leave them. But she ran, because it was the only way.

"Exactly," I said, when I caught my breath. "That's it, girls. You're never alone anywhere. Not really. But you can be lonely almost anywhere, too."

When I looked back at Nora's pictures from that night,
I really wanted to see some paranormal shit, possibly
more than I've ever really wanted to before. The photos
are extraordinary. K and D running so fast and so grace-
fully, like pink- and blue-haired fawns, midair, one
slender hoof attached to the earth, arms stretched up to
the night sky, caught in Nora's artificial light from a box.
Sometimes I'm there, too, far in the background, my arms
folded across my body as if I'm trying to keep myself on the
ground. There's one close up, a profile; I'm looking down
at the ground with my hands stuffed deep in my jacket
pockets, my nose wrinkled and set off by the cascade of hair
falling in a blur on the other side of my face.

"I think you sneezed," Nora says, as we're passing the
camera around in the Waffle House late that night.

"I think it's my favorite picture ever," I say, and we
huddle close in the booth.

"So who did die in the fire? Did anybody?" K wants to
know.

"And which fire?" I tell K and D and Nora that they
should look all this up, that the history is pretty well-
recorded. There are people who are still alive who grew
up with the nuns and priests there. Lots of people whose
parents grew up there and who heard stories. I tell them
one of the fires had started as a priest was trying to get rid
of some wasps' nests and the wasps caught on fire—I was in
the middle of trying to explain, destruction of property,
but no deaths, when they all burst out with,

"Flaming Wasps!"

"Now that's actually scary." K was still trying to salvage
some legitimate drama in the evening.

"So." I said. "I guess I can tell you a really scary story. And it happened to me, so you know it's true. But you've got to promise me not to tell it yourself unless you thank him. In some way. Make him look good, you know? Because even though it's a scary story, and even though he's a ghost, it's really a story about a hero..." It is a great story, and even though I might have lost them at flaming wasps, the only thing left to do was to give it a shot...

CHAPTER SEVENTEEN

I HAD TO TELL THOMAS that I need to take a break from
the photo experiments for a while. Some photographs have
as much power as a place, I'm finding. And I'm finding
that I need to be careful. I thought they were windows, the
frames around the edges. But sometimes they're doors.

Ha. My father used to say that to me—"You make a
better door than you do a window." He'd say it when I was
blocking his view of the television.

I left some doors open. I was reading again, checking my
work. I found out one thing about Justine—her photographer turned out to be a famous director years after he
took her picture. Maybe that's why it looks like a story.
Cinematic. Maybe that's all it is. A little movie in my head.

Justine packs a bag. She keeps packing, but every time
she turns around, there's something else. She decides not
to take the perfume bottles her grandmother left, because
she's afraid they'll leak on her books. On her clothes. It
wasn't worth it; at least one of the bottles was sour.

The front door downstairs slammed. She was trying to
finish and be gone before either of them got back from
work. She wasn't really that afraid. She was old enough that
if he hit her again, she could go to the police. The police
might not always be friendly to her, but they wouldn't look
well on him particularly, either. She figured they were
about even in that respect.

It wasn't him at all; it was her mother. She could tell
from the footfalls—her mother wore heavy boots to work,
too, but her step was closer and lighter than his. She went
into the kitchen, so Justine took her bag, crossed the room

and left, leaving anything that hadn't gone into the bag. Some shoes. The perfume bottles. Nothing that mattered.

"So will you have some bread to take? There's some cheese, too."

"I'll be alright. I don't want to put you into trouble later."

"It's my bread, too, isn't it? I pay for half." Her mother bit off a piece of the loaf in her hand, and Justine couldn't help laughing. She couldn't help crying a little, too. She hadn't really meant for things to end up as they were. Mostly she worried about leaving her mother, and leaving Roberta, her little sister. Her mother's husband, Roberta's father and Justine's stepfather, was no good. He was not even a good stereotype. Not a drinker. Just mean.

All he'd needed to kick Justine out of the house was a decent excuse, and her friends provided it. "Why do you all dress that way?" her mother used to ask, "What does it mean?" And then one day the Beast reads an article in the evening paper about the youth gangs in Edwardian clothes, and it's shouting before dinner, shouting until there's no dinner, her mother crying in the kitchen and telling her to get out as well, feeling betrayed that she hadn't confided in her.

It was just something to do, Justine thought. Boring Americans, boring shortages, boring school—she was tired of the things her parents seemed to celebrate so much. They had no imagination, and they didn't care about anything, except that they'd been saved from the war. That's great that we're still alive, Justine thought, but now what do we do? Sit around and listen to the radio. Read about sports in the papers.

She'd get out. It couldn't be any worse, really. She stayed at Myra's house three days a week as it was. They both had jobs at the theater on the weekends. She thought maybe that's what she'd want to do one day, be an actress. If she ever got a chance to do anything so silly. Right now she had to survive. And have fun. Because if she couldn't have some fun in the meantime, there wasn't really any point to surviving.

"I'll take the bread," Justine reached out, and her mother took her hand in hers.

"I'm sorry," she said. "I'm sorry, but you understand? Why you have to go? It's not my fault, now, don't you see?"

Justine pulled her hand free from her mother's, took up her bag and left the kitchen, striding through the living room to the front entry. By the door, she caught sight of herself in the mirror, her grandmother's pin shining in her lapel, and for a second she smiled at the sight of it. Then she walked through the doorway for the last time.

Myra found her at the record store. "He wants to meet you, Justine. Let's go—"

"Who? Where are we going?"

"That photographer I told you about, remember? He's coming back. We told him there'd be more of us later, and he said he'd come back." Myra was so gullible, Justine thought. What would she have to save her from this time? A photographer.

"What sort of creep is he, then? Taking pictures of girls? Is that what he's after?"

"No, no. He says he came to take pictures of the boys—"

"Oh, *well.*"

"No, the *teddies*. He asked us all about what kind of music we like and where we hang out. Stuff like that. He thinks it's interesting. He writes for the newspaper. Says he thought it was all boys, didn't know about the girls—"

"Well, he must be pretty stupid. Anywhere there's boys, there's girls."

"That's it?" Myra said, looking at Justine's bag. Her grandmother's old carpet bag. Really more of a giant purse.

"I don't have anything that's mine," Justine said, hefting the bag a little with one gray gloved hand.

"Look at the new sign," Myra nodded to the back wall of the record store, where a big placard had been placed reading, "No Edwardian Dress."

"Bum lickers. Who's gonna buy these, then?" Justine dropped the 45 back into its sleeve. Eddie Cochrane. She laughed and grabbed Myra by the arm. They ran past the clerk at the register, and Justine sang out to him, in her deepest register, "I'd like to help ya, son, but cha too young to vote! Hahahaha! Ya too young!" She shook her finger at him, and he put his hands up on the counter as if about to turn them out of the store, but they were gone already, the little bells tinkling behind them as the door swung back to shut.

"'We won the war, hurray!' That's all they think they ever had to do. They just sit around now cause they got it all figured and everything is perfect. Look at this mess. We don't have anything that's not broken." Justine pointed to the rubble-filled lots that still dotted the street between the half-repaired buildings.

"Let's go get our pictures taken," Justine said. "Why not? That's the only way anyone's ever going to remember who we are."

The movie stops, the tea kettle is shrieking. *I have to be more careful. The chakra meditation thing isn't working. They're getting inside.*

CHAPTER EIGHTEEN

"I SEE YOU SURVIVED TRADER JOE'S." Thomas greeted me and took the bags, dropping them on the kitchen counter.

"Please punch me in the face the next time I say I'm going there on a Saturday." I say that every time I go. Maybe I should take him with me and put him on a cart. With boxing gloves. Or a javelin.

"What's so great in there, anyway?"

I stop to think. It's a worthwhile question. Why do I knock myself out to go to a place that purposefully designs parking lots like MC Escher dorm room posters? With aisles like one-way country bridges in blind road bends? Where all the food names are sufficiently clever and unfamiliar so that each shopper has to stop and scrutinize every food label like it's an acrostic composed of Linear B?

"I mean, what's in the bag?" Thomas the Engineer goes for the concrete question, since I'm having a little trouble spitting out a snappy answer.

"Let's see. Oatmeal. Yogurt."

"Well, you sure can't get that stuff anyplace else."

"Not wholegrain blueberry oatmeal with flax seeds. And it's the only one Edgar likes."

"*Now* it is."

And there you have it, see. Going to Trader Joe's that first time is like shooting up heroin for the first time. It's not casual. You don't do it by accident. Somebody told you that they see what your problem is, and they know just how to fix it. They know how to fill that hole in your soul.

And it's going to be filled with mushroom turnovers and shelf-stable whipping cream and bourbon maple syrup. It's the Hotel California of supermarkets. You can check out any time you like, but you can never leave.

They're so nice in there, too. The staff—not the shoppers. The shoppers are just junkies. Like you.

And, there's cheap alcohol.

"Also, I have those pigs in a blanket—the ones in the phyllo—"

"Oh. Those are good."

"These crackers shaped like cats—"

It's what happens. They get you, and suddenly it's only that particular tasting oatmeal. You put your own flax seeds in, but it's just not the same. It all tastes... a little better.

But you pay. You pay on the way in and on the way out, and I'm not talking about the cash register. It's a confrontation with the dark side of humanity. Parking spaces. Carts. The last box of chocolate dipped peppermint Joe's Os. Old ladies will cut you. Young women will cut you. They use their children as battering rams.

"It was so packed today the staff was playing some *Classic Rawk*."

On the bright side, Trader Joe's is normally spirit-free. It's quite remarkable. *Normally*. Is it possible that I can still use that word without irony? I get funny looks at home.

"Was the music driving out the North Raleigh matrons?"

"No, they were too committed to pumpkin-related items. I think some were camped there waiting for the shipment of Advent calendars to be unloaded. I think it was mostly agitating them."

"Not jamming in the aisles to 'Livin' On a Prayer,' were they?"

"Oh no—the lightest thing I heard was Ratt's 'Round and Round.' I think I'll forever hear the classic AC/DC number 'Back in Black' as 'Brie En Croute.' Because I got one of those, too. Who's got time to make one from scratch? I do have a fantastic cranberry sauce recipe that's going to really set it off..." I paused for a minute, because the earworm was back. The only way to get rid of an earworm is to replace all the lyrics. I tried singing it out.

"Brie en croute! Put on a suit! Get out your tie and try to look cute, y'all, I got Fancy snacks, in my sack, preheat the stove and get out some crack-ers..."

Thomas just stared. No air guitar, no hair flip.

So I changed trajectory. "Did I dream this, or do you have an ex-girlfriend who designed parking lots? Because I'm pretty sure the overhead view of every Trader Joe's parking lot is a question mark followed by a middle finger."

"That's right! I almost forgot about her. Well, not about her, but about the parking lot thing. Yeah, she had some stuff to work out, now that you mention it."

"There ought to be a screening process for that sort of thing before those people go into any kind of municipal design. I see evidence of some sort of punitive campaign. Perhaps she's working things out."

"Oh, I bought you a present." Thomas produced a brown paper sack and drew out a bottle of Evan Williams egg nog. "I know it's a little early in the season," he said, "but I was in the liquor store, and it made me think of you."

"Ah, baby, *you thought of me in the liquor store.* Those might be the most romantic words in English. I'll take some of that right now, actually."

"That bad at the Trader Joe's—really?" Thomas was already getting out the glasses.

"Well, besides the hell of marketing, I did have something else come up."

"A little unexpected mental movie? I'm sorry; I'm sure the timing wasn't great on that."

"I really thought it was just the mega-stress I was picking up, but somebody in there today had... an appendage."

People can be haunted, just like places.

"I brushed up against somebody. I mean, you always brush up against somebody in Trader Joe's, but somewhere in the awkward negotiation of leaving behind my cart and trying to carry four bags in two hands so I didn't have to play chicken across the kitty-cornered, psychotically-arranged islands to return the thing after dragging it all the way to my car, I collided with someone I didn't see."

That's every Trader Joe's, from LA to North Raleigh. Between the register and the cart corral, there are so many strangers in so many narrow aisles, it's an array of inappropriate public contact. It's like a slow rave, a techno dance party with brown bags and red carts. Everybody's waving hands in the air, swinging their hips back and forth. Or maybe the chain was started by unemployed social scientists who could never get that grant to build life-sized mazes for *people.*

"So once I congratulated myself for balancing the bags so that I'd reduced the number of parking lot crossings by half, drastically increasing my chances of survival, I realized I'd picked up something else, hanging on like when you walk through a cloud of bad seventies floral perfume like White Linen, that old lady hairspray smell."

"Ugh."

"Except it wasn't a smell, exactly. It just held on like that."

"No, I got you. Still revolting."

"It was. It was an ugly, twisted kind of feeling. And it was fresh, like somebody had just gotten sprayed with it. Sense memory."

"That's bound to happen in Trader Joe's. All those samples."

Oh God; it did make sense. There's all kinds of memory fire-starters in there. Flowers, cookies, fruit smells. Hawaiian Shirts. Good lord—they even ring a great big ship's bell.

"And you didn't see who it was?" Thomas had found the box of tiny peanut butter cups in the last bag and was wrangling the cellophane off of it.

"No. I mean, I probably saw the person. I saw like five thousand people trying to get in or out. But I didn't know when I saw him. Or her. Or that. You know, that there was this thing."

"It was a thing? You don't usually call it a 'thing.' But then again, what do you call them? Because you don't like that word 'ghost'—I see you tense up whenever anybody says it."

"'Thing' works here. It was nasty. A mean thing, a lot of angry with a bunch of sad on the bottom. And it came in there *with* somebody, because it didn't belong to that space."

Thomas looked kind of funny eating dainty little peanut butter cups. Especially with such a serious look. Bourbon and chocolate taste disgusting together, to me at least. But he seemed content, so I went on.

"It was heavy, too. So I guess to most people it looked like my bags were too heavy, but then, after I got the bags in the car, I guess I was sort of leaning on the back door having a little head-on-my-desk moment, and I heard somebody ask me if I was okay. I think that's what he asked me."

That wasn't what he asked me. I dropped the bags into the back of the Cube, shut the door and then leaned there for a second. It would have all looked perfectly normal if I'd been smoking a cigarette, for instance. But I heard this voice—heard him before I saw him. He said, "It looks like you're having a fugue state. Are you having a fugue state?"

I still had a lot of angry old gray scratchy thing hanging over me, so once I located the man in the trench coat with the bag from Jerry's Artarama, I looked up and said, "What the hell are you, the psychiatric incarnation of that Microsoft paperclip?"

"Look, I know it's going to sound a little strange, but your brain is telling me you're having a fugue state."

"Well, you're mistaken. And if only, by the way, that were the problem."

"So if it isn't a fugue state, do you mind me asking what it is? Because you're ruining a near-perfect record, so it'd be a help to me to know, kinda, where I went wrong. For data aggregation purposes."

I couldn't place his accent. Not many people only sound *kind* of Southern. And his diction wasn't Southern. Just the occasional elongated vowel sound. He raised his shaggy eyebrows and shrugged, waving the bag a little.

"It's... ah, you're not gonna like this answer. It's not easy to explain."

"Still sounding like a fugue state, but whatever. And I don't like or dislike answers to questions. As long as they are real answers."

"Okay then. Remember, you wanted to know. And this is in fact a Real Answer for you."

I explained to him pretty explicitly and directly that on the way out of the Trader Joe's, I had been accosted by what seemed to be somebody's dead step-parent, in-law, or possibly a teacher or mentor figure with a serious, serious vendetta. *Oh, I realized, that's it. He got away with something.*

"Got away with what?"

"I don't know. That's the problem, see. All I get is this big wave of emotion, like I just read a whole novel, a ten-novel series. Like I just listened to a five-act opera. Sang a five-act opera. But in the span of a second. It's like that. Times a thousand. But sometimes, it's actually *severe.*"

He crossed his arms. The trench coat was pretty old, had a lot of what looked like paint or ink or something.

"So, you talk to dead people?"

"No, I don't. That is not at all what I do. I don't talk to any of these things. Except when I say, 'The rule is no manifestions,' or 'I am trying, but you're gonna have to be more clear.'"

"That's too bad, because I was going to say 'What a coincidence! I, in fact, talk to the living.'"

I had misjudged him, it seemed. "Oh, you're *way* more annoying than the paperclip."

I had stopped telling the story. Thomas was constructing what looked like a kind of graph out of the empty peanut butter cup wrappers. He'd slide one up, another to the side, occasionally jumping over other wrappers in short hops. "One time, the girl who designed the parking lots? One time she woke me up in the middle of the night to pray for me."

I thought about it for a second. I didn't make a joke, though.

"That's a gift, of sorts," I said. And he nodded. Deep down, I wondered what it would look like, to pray for Thomas. He deserved a person who could do that for him. I mean, effectively. Like, with any expectation of result.

Chapter Nineteen

"IF I WERE TO DESCRIBE my worst fears of what I sound like to other people, that's about it." Thomas had asked me to describe the man in the trench coat, using concrete words other than "man," "trench coat" and "weird."

"So then he kind of swans around and says 'I'm sorry if I sounded facetious; that wasn't my intent. Of course I don't mean that I chitty-chat with the living, the way everybody else does. I receive communications from souls and minds that are not articulated externally.' And he was kind of swaying a little, almost, like he was dancing to his own monologue. Then I asked him if he read minds or something."

"Oh no. Is this like the psychic fair thing again?"

"No, he said that's not it."

He never really did clarify, though, on that point. So I had a hard time explaining it to Thomas, the rest of the conversation.

I was still kind of gesturing toward my car door with my keys, envisioning extraction. But I was the one who kept on. "It *sounds* an awful lot like mind-reading. I'm thinking of a card..."

"And I'm thinking of my dead aunt Helen. How does she feel about my new hat?"

I hadn't noticed his hat before. It was ridiculous. Houndstooth. I didn't need to consult dead aunt Helen.

"Okay, so we both have complicated situations." How could I not have noticed the hat?

"Right. And you're not having a fugue state, it seems. But you've had them? You know what I'm talking about?"

It had been a while, but I definitely knew what he was talking about.

"I used to find bodies of water." See? I could have left then, but I kept on talking.

"All right then. Yes. So. Is it like that? When they tell you things?"

"Maybe. More like a panic attack, I always thought. But I don't really know for sure. Once in a while I don't even really remember—" I thought about that day with Edgar, the bowls. There had been a good five, maybe ten minutes I lost that morning. I described it to him.

"Interesting. I've never met anyone with these kinds of episodes. I need to go now, but I'd like to discuss this further. Here is my card. Wait, I don't have a card with me. Give me your hand."

He pulled out a felt marker with one hand and took my left hand up with the other. He wrote something; I could feel the pen curve and sweep, like he was drawing the lines of my palm. Then he stalked off toward the lower end of the parking lot, past Trader Joe's, disappearing between crisscrossing Expeditions.

"Huh. Weird." Thomas refilled the glasses, first his, then mine. We were drinking out of our Smurf glasses. "What's it say on your hand?"

"That's the other thing," I said, and I held out my left hand for Thomas to inspect.

Nothing *that* messed up can happen when you're drinking good liquor out of glasses with Smurfs on them.

"Jeebus."

"I know." The markings on my hand were very elegant, and there were a few numbers in there.

"I don't know, Nic. He didn't say his name?"

"I don't think so. I don't remember. I'm certain he's harmless."

"Strange man in a parking lot."

"I know."

"In a trench coat."

"See? It's almost too much of a stereotype to be dangerous, really."

Thomas still looked uncomfortable, but he nodded.

"Keep an eye out for him, though."

"No doubt."

"Hey, let me see that hand again. Take a picture?"

"Sure. I think that one is some kind of printer's symbol," I pointed to a thing that looked like a flower petal. Or a stylized dagger, maybe. Thomas held his phone hovering over my palm.

I *was* sure I had not written it. Really sure.

"Got it," he said. He smiled, you know, to be reassuring.

CHAPTER TWENTY

YOU MAKE A BETTER DOOR, you make a better door. I'm dreaming. My father's voice is coming out of an old television. I make a better door than a window. Someone is at the door, climbing in. It's not real; it's just a picture. It's not a real girl. Just a girl in a picture.

Justine clambered through the rubble after Myra. They were cutting through an abandoned ruin, making their way back to the alley where Myra's friend the photographer had been taking pictures earlier and had promised to return.

"He's not my *friend*, Justine. I just met him."

"But you let him take pictures of you. Some man whose name you don't even know."

"How's knowing a name going to make anything safer? I know a lot of names," Myra laughed curtly and shrugged. "And his name is Kenneth. Ken."

"Kenneth Ken?"

"Oh come off it. Ken. Ken something with an S. No, with an R. What does it matter. If you didn't want to come, you shoulda said so."

Justine felt bad for getting Myra flustered. It was a bad day, but it wasn't Myra's fault. And she didn't mind having her picture taken. When she was a little girl, she had once been taken to a photographer's studio with her mother. She must have been nearly a baby; the little bits she remembered were brief and out-of-place. She remembered sitting in a green velvet chair with an ornate oval back, almost falling asleep while her mother brushed her hair with a big, soft brush. Or was it in the taxi that she almost fell asleep? Where had her father been? She remembered sitting in her mother's lap for the pictures taken by a man in the darkness somewhere away from them while they sat in the bright light. All she saw was her mother's face, her shining eyes, then the blindness, momentary after each flash. During the first bombings, she had run through the house shouting that giants were taking pictures of the world. Her father slapped her before hurrying them all into the basement. She didn't make that mistake again.

She giggled and hopped across to Myra, who had climbed up onto a half-torn down stone wall. They could follow it through the back of the lot all the way over to the next block. One foot in front of the other, she placed her right hand on her friend's shoulder, not so much for balance.

Justine faked a pout and said, "I'm sorry, girl. It sounds like fun, and anyway, what else would we be doing? What'd you tell this guy about us already?"

"Told him we were queens. Perfect. That nobody messes with us."

"Ladies, then. I'll get my manners out."

"Oh, he was right impressed, I think. He's coming back. Jack told him there were lots more."

"Jack? Who else was there?"

"Petey and Richard. Barbara, Pat... Jack told him there were lots more of us. Oh look."

Myra bent down and stretched one foot then the other onto the broken ends of the wall, coming down into the side street. Justine could hear Eileen's voice already.

"What do we care? I don't even remember a time when

everything wasn't broken. None of us do."

I do, thought Justine, but she knew she was a couple of years older than Eileen, and anyway she didn't feel like fighting about anything else today.

"Hellooo kids," Myra skipped up, pulling Justine by the hand behind her. "Ken, this is Justine, the girl I told you about, my friend."

He was a lot younger than Justine had thought he'd be, and she didn't like the looks of him at first. He had pale hair and his eyes were terrifying. The way he looked at all of them—like he was at the beach, collecting shells.

"Justine! Yes. Thank you so much for coming." He held out a hand to shake hers. It struck her as curious, his manner, as if he had called them all to a meeting in their own yard.

"Nowhere else to be. This is it."

"Well then. I'm going to set up a tripod over here. But just carry on as you normally would. I'll keep asking you questions, though, if that's okay."

Justine wasn't sure if it was okay or not. Nobody ever asked them questions.

"What kinds of questions, Mister?"

Ken bristled and smiled all at once in what seemed like a very different way. Still, Justine couldn't tell if it was better or worse. Who was this person? What could he possibly want from them?

"Are you a dancer?"

"*That's* the best question you've got?"

"Ha. They said you were the toughest one. But I think you look like a dancer."

"Hey, nobody said she was the *toughest*. But she's tough, because she's one of us." Jack came over and put his arm around Justine, protective and brotherly, but puffing himself up at the same time. They had all grown up together, most of them. Jack and Petey, his little sister Rosie. Eileen. Myra. Richard had moved from South-ampton a couple years back, right about the time they had started wearing these long coats and high collars, piling their hair and slicking it down. Nobody planned it. Nobody read it in a book.

"Justine is a dancer." Myra grabbed Justine and swung her around, they spun and Myra twirled.

"I'm serious." Ken walked over and spoke lower to Justine. "Didn't mean to offend. I studied ballet myself, is all. You walk like a dancer."

Justine softened her scowl a little, but she rolled her shoulders and pulled a pack of cigarettes out of her deep jacket pocket. She held the pack toward Ken. At first he backed away, but he glanced up with his eyes—like an animal, but she couldn't place it yet. A fox? Then he leaned in and took a cigarette, quickly and lightly. She hardly saw or felt the motion at all, but he already dangled the cigarette from his goofy smile. That smile. She felt like he put it there to cancel out the look of his sharp eyes.

"I never danced ballet. Never even seen a ballet."

"Oh. Well, you'd be great, I bet. Do you mind if I take your picture, just right now while you're standing there?"

"Wouldn't have come here at all if I minded. Myra said you wanted to take pictures of us. I don't know if I understand why. Nobody else is interested in us. What are you after?"

"I can tell you're a smart girl. Shouldn't trust a man with a camera and no story. I'm writing for a magazine. *Picture Post.* You know it?"

"Course I know it. My dad used to read it. Before the war." He stopped, though, after he got back. Maybe stopped reading altogether. Maybe he never read it at all—she only saw the stacks of the old issues her mother had kept while her father was away fighting. And when he came back, no reading, just shouting. She used to think it wasn't really even him, the man who came back. She heard her mother say to the neighbor Mrs. Cheatham once, "He's not the same man who left here to go to war. He's not the same!" That day, when he came home, Justine refused to kiss his cheek, screaming "What have you done with my real father?" Things were never quite the same after. Then he left, and her mother married the Beast.

"Are you going to take my picture? You're just staring at me."

Ken raised the camera and snapped. Not just once, many times. She lost count.

"So why the drainpipe pants and the coats? What's the message?"

"The message is we look good," Jack said, straightening Petey's tie.

"I mean, what are you nostalgic for? Before the war? Before the other war? We weren't even born then. I'm only twenty-five, and you kids seem older and younger than me at the same time. What are you looking for?"

"We're not *looking* for anything. There isn't anything. There's just right now. Everything is gone. The people before us—our parents, our grandparents, they all used everything up." Justine thought about her mother, how worried her mother's face was when she left. Not about what would happen to her. Just what would happen if she wasn't gone before her father got home, like he had insisted she be.

Ken had brought them a box of sandwiches. Justine sat down on a low wall with one, unwrapping the wax paper. He walked over and started taking apart his camera, changing out lenses, checking settings.

"Did he hit you? Your dad?"

Justine coughed a little on the bite of sandwich. "Who are you?"

"Look, it's not that hard to see. My father did. He beat me every day for years. I can tell when somebody's got a shit like that at home. You can tell, can't you?"

"No. No, I can't. I don't know. I don't think about it. It's none of my business! And none of yours. Don't you write any of that."

"I have no intention of writing about that. I won't even use your name if you'd rather not."

"Why are you even asking, then." She felt his eyes again, like tweezers, poking and peeling.

"I won't bother you about it. Really, I just—it was the same with me is all. Are you out yet?" Myra was looking over. Justine refused to cry.

"Today," she said. "Myra took me in. Everything I have is in this bag."

"Everything you have is *not* in that bag," Ken said. This

time, she believed him.

They sat on the rocks for a while eating sandwiches.

She started the questions this time. "So you used to be a ballet dancer. Is that why your dad—"

"No, I don't think he cared about that. There wasn't any reason. There isn't ever any real reason, you know. Twats. They're bigger, so they do. They're in a pain they can't bear, so they give it away, they think they can escape it that way. They hit you because they don't understand sacrifice."

He was thinking of it, she thought. He's thinking about him. She was thinking about her father. At first she didn't know what Ken meant, that they didn't understand sacrifice, but as the memory of her father, his face twisted, his fist drawn back—as the image emerged, she knew.

"But no, he didn't seem to notice much of what I did. And then I went into the navy, and that was mostly the end of my ballet career."

"You were in the navy? Not during the war."

"End of the war. I was young."

Justine wasn't sure she wanted to know badly enough to ask. You don't ask people about the war to be polite. He went on as if she had spoken out.

"Of course, yes, it was not a happy experience. I was in the Pacific. I was more afraid of my commanding officer than I was of the Japanese. I never saw one; the war was over by the time I got anywhere. The fact that it was over already made the cruelty just absurd. Other people—" Ken stopped and fumbled around in his pockets, "Other people had it worse. Of course. Say, could I have another of those..."

Justine took out the pack and shook a cigarette free into his hand. He smiled.

"Will you leave school, then?"

"Why? Oh, I don't know. If I can get a full shift, I suppose I will. It's not as if it will matter much."

"What do you want to do?"

Justine glanced up. "I don't know. Later we'll all go down the dance hall in Walthamstow..."

Ken laughed. "No, no; I mean, what do you want to do *one day*? If you could do anything."

Justine tried to decide whether or not to be honest. She didn't put a lot of thought in these kinds of things. She didn't know at all what she wanted to do. Only what she didn't want to do.

"I don't want to get married and have some sap's pack of kids. Cook up dinner every night. Get old."

"You're awfully young to worry about getting old."

"How old are you? Not very. Why take pictures of a bunch of stupid kids in no place going nowhere? What do you want to do? You're a long way from the ballet. Or the navy, for that matter."

Ken thought. "I guess that's true enough."

He stared off at the kids chasing each other under the metal supports from a new building that had been started and left unfinished. Maybe that was why they came here, this unfinished building. A broken promise. Doorframes and windowsills, windows and doors. The kids go in and out the broken/unfinished windows.

I'm on the edge of the window, in black and white. The ground below me. Am I inside? I can hear Edgar's voice but it's far away. He's looking for his shoes to go outside. We're already outside, I think. Don't go near the window, I tell him. I can't see him. I only see Ken, because Justine is looking at him carefully.

"But I started taking pictures in the navy, and—well, it's going to sound strange I guess. Sometimes it reminded me of the things I liked when I was dancing."

Something about the awkwardness of his confession, his perception that it was awkward, made Justine laugh, but not the superior, mean laugh they usually practiced on each other, she and her friends. It was a funny thing to say. Even funnier was that she was almost certain she knew what he meant. And then it struck her as completely hilarious that he was completely unlikely to believe her.

"Oh, I'm not laughing at you. Well, a little, but I'm laughing at myself. When I was eight years old, I tried to tell my best friend that I could see colors when I looked at the alphabet letters on the classroom wall. She told the teacher, and I got in trouble."

Ken looked serious. "You're right, though. Some people do see things like that. When they hear musical notes, they actually see colors. Did you know that? You know the Blues? Why do you think they call it a 'blue' note? Some people can see it. Not everybody can. That's the trouble, though. The ones that can't see it will try to tell you it's not there."

He really did look young. She found it hard to believe he had been in the war at all.

"I had this dream once. It was a long time ago, but…" She wasn't sure why she was telling him this, but she had started talking as soon as it occurred to her, so she kept going. She had never told anyone, held onto it for years, waited for it to return even though it never had. "I was in a place like here, open, the ground covered with piles of blocks." Because she had never put the dream into words, she felt like a small child struggling with concepts bigger than her language. What she said out loud didn't make sense. She didn't know if she could describe it so that he could see it. "Blocks, about the size of these rocks over here, you know. Big enough to stand on. All of them were either bright blue or bright yellow."

Ken smoked and listened intently, those fox-like eyes a little softer now, but still taking her in piece by piece.

"And I was stepping on them. Bouncing, a little, because instead of hard, like rocks or blocks, they were spongy, springy. Just when I landed on them. The edges were hard, but when I jumped onto each one, it pushed me a little to the next." She paused. "And as it pushed, it made a tone. A musical note. Except—" The words stopped. How to talk about a sound you don't hear? "I didn't hear the music. I could feel it. Like... like the way a string inside a piano feels. When someone hits a key. I guess that's what it would be like."

Ken nodded for a while. "You had this dream more than once?"

"Just once," she said, apologetically. "A long time ago."

"It's a beautiful dream to remember. Do you think about it when you listen to music?"

"Always," she said, even before she could decide whether or not that was the right answer.

"Say, what are they doing over there? Under that—what is it, scaffolding?"

"Oh, they were putting up a new building but they never—that's Jack and Petey."

"Do they—is that a gun? Do they have guns?"

"Oh, please," Justine stood up and cupped one hand over her eyes to shade from the sun that had started to go down. "Jack! What are you doing?"

Justine saw Eileen come out from behind the low wall. She stared with her hands in her pockets, then waved up at them both.

Justine started down the slope of debris, Ken following right behind. "What are they doing, Eileen? Are those guns?"

"Yeah, aren't they lovely? Pearl-handled. Dueling pistols."

"What are we dueling over, Jack?"

"I dunno, Petey. What do you say?"

"Well, not Eileen I'd say."

"Yes, surely not Eileen."

"Bugger off, you both." Eileen folded her arms. She had a new jacket, too, white with black piping. Justine tried not to be distracted, though.

"What'd you go and give them those for, Eileen? You know they're like as not to hurt themselves."

"So?" Eileen just shrugged and ran over to Jack. They stood back to back, Jack pointing the actual gun at Petey and Eileen making a gun shape with her fingers, but standing perfectly straight, the sharp cut of her overcoat making her into a striking geometric figure, more architecture than girl.

"Stop it, all of you," Justine called out. She tried to sound detached and bored by it all, but Ken heard the quaver as she finished.

"Hang on, boys," Ken trotted out in between them, holding his hands to the sides. "Don't shoot. Let me have a look for a sec. This'll make a great shot for the piece. Let me take a quick look at this weapon you have here." Ken walked over to Petey, who offered the elaborate handle of the pistol. Ken tilted his head, turned the gun to one side and opened the chamber, cleared the passage. He smiled and returned it to Petey, who gripped the handle and made a clumsy attempt to flip it back around into his palm.

Ken leaned toward Justine as he ran back up the incline to retrieve his camera. "Not loaded; don't worry. I'll check the other, too. Just wait."

Justine watched the whole tableau uncomfortably while Ken set up a tripod and finally made his way over to Jack, who meanwhile practiced his draw from his coat pocket, flapping like a water bird. What were they all doing here, anyway. Ken looked over and gave her a nod no one else noticed as he arranged Jack into an elegant stance. Petey mirrored him, and Ken placed Eileen between them, in the foreground, her arms folded across her chest.

He stood back and looked at them through the camera. "Wait," he called out. From the pile of camera equipment, he pulled out an umbrella and placed it in Eileen's hand.

"Stand it here, that's right. And then cross your leg at the knee and point this foot—exactly."

It was perfect. Eileen's jacket slanted off-kilter. Everything about to fall down.

"Wait, Jack," Petey called out, mournfully. "Why are we *dueling*?"

"*Sacrifice!*" Justine called out across the rubble.

Ken's camera clicked.

The door opened.

"Mommy fell down," Edgar tells Thomas.

"I see," says Thomas.

Chapter Twenty One

I STARTED MEETING WITH Trench Coat man pretty regularly. He was still kind of abrasive, but was too good a source of information to pass up. I couldn't Google the kind of expert supernaturalism he offered up in each visit, and while I might not be buying all of what he was selling, I felt like I was getting some worthwhile tidbits to ponder.

"I've started to believe, after all these years, that I might be compulsively driven toward liminal beings. Like an insect circling itself toward the light."

"I'm a liminal being?"

"Of course. You're like... a portal. A door."

I kind of snorted because it was all sounding so hokey, and I was tired.

"But I'd rather have met you under less, well, *creepy* circumstances. Could I possibly talk to your husband for a moment?"

"Thomas?

"Thomas! Yes, Thomas."

"What, like, on the phone?"

"Lacking anything more expedient. Can you bring him up on Facetime? I'd rather see him—and I'm sure he'd rather see me." Abrasive isn't even the right word. A little unctuous, maybe.

It was mostly serendipity when I found him again. I was in Jerry's Artarama one day with Nora re-stocking Copic markers and micron pens, and it occurred to me that he had been coming out of Jerry's that day I met him, and that such a figure might stick with the Artarama folks. They always knew Nora, even though I was pretty sure she wasn't the only purpled haired teenager shopping in Jerry's.

"Ben?" the girls at the counter said to each other, "Is she talking about the guy in the coat? He's in here at least once a week. Does he, like, paint? I don't know? Maybe something with like woodworking? I don't know?" One of them had a piercing on her upper lip. The placement was unfortunate; I kept wanting to straighten it for her. The other had spectacular gauges, each one a Victorian-styled picture frame bearing a portrait. Two different portraits. I leaned sideways to get a view to make sure.

But I didn't ever even get a chance to look for him at Jerry's. I ran into him at Cup a Joe, only a few days later, I think. "Who do you mean? Over there? In here all the time. Yeah." Randy, the barista at Cup a Joe, seemed a little surprised at my reaction to seeing Ben roosted like a hen in his crumpled trench coat reading the paper at the table in the front window.

"I guess I just haven't been in here at the same time…" Seemed a little unlikely, given my devotion to my daily coffee, sometimes twice daily coffee… But anyway, there he was, and everyone else seemed to be quite accustomed to his hulking presence. They hardly took any notice of him at all.

I called Thomas on the telephone while I was waiting for my latte. "Randy knows him?"

"Says he's been in here all the time."

I couldn't put a name to my suspicion.

"Oh well, then. I've probably seen him. There's a whole

troop of regulars. Anyway, you're in Cup a Joe; I'm sure it's fine. Do you think he could be helpful? I mean, it seems like he might have some information for you."

I wasn't sure. About any part of *help*. Whether I needed it or whether it could be had in any form. But it was consoling, I admitted, to talk to somebody else who picked things up they couldn't control and couldn't explain. Even if it wasn't exactly the same thing. So we kept meeting for coffee, once or twice a week. I figured, what could go wrong at Cup a Joe's.

So sitting across from Ben, I tried calling Thomas again. "I just talked to him. Maybe he's driving. He might not pick up if he's driving."

"Certainly. Prudent man."

"Anyway, you guys probably have seen each other in here, since you're in here..."

"Oh, constantly." Ben looked over, and I couldn't help but wonder if he was picking something up. Then I couldn't help but wonder if Thomas felt that way sitting across from me sometimes. "You're fortunate, you know," he said. "Having someone to help you watch out for things."

"I know—" I began, then stopped. "I was just thinking about—"

"No, no," he said, waving a hand lightly. "That was an entirely external observation. Nothing emanating. You'd probably know, I'm betting."

I laughed. It was a weird feeling. I also felt a little sad, because as near as I could tell so far, it would seem that maybe Ben did not have anyone to help him "watch out for things," as he said.

"I am fortunate," I said, "but I asked, finally. I'd have never had help if I hadn't asked. But it's true I might not have asked if I hadn't been pretty sure of being understood."

"How long?"

"Oh, I was in my forties. Before I ever said it out loud."

"Ah."

"I was told... not to tell anyone."

"That's what Grandpas always say, isn't it. Did he say it would be your *special secret?*"

I scowled at him. "I didn't even know myself. I mean, I knew what happened to me sometimes. But I didn't name it as a regular part of me." I felt like I wasn't making much sense, but Ben could practically finish my sentences.

"You thought you were mentally ill."

That was probably an external observation, too. But it was hard to think about. I guess I had thought so. Worse, I guess my mother maybe thought so. I know several of my exes thought so. I told him that my first husband was an experimental psychologist and lobbied hard for medication.

"I might have listened to him and taken something, but I'd already been down that road, in high school."

"You went on what? Paxil? Wellbutrin?"

"I can't remember what it was called. It was a Valium derivative. It was 1982, though. Limited options."

"And you took it."

"I was fifteen."

"You wanted to get better. Did you?"

"Take it?"

"No. Did you get better?"

Well, of course I got better, because I'm here. But if I got better, it was in spite of treatment, not because of. The meds I was supposed to take every day at four in the afternoon wiped me out for the rest of the day. I remembered lying on the floor of my teenage room, the phone ringing and ringing. No voicemail back then. Just ringing and ringing. I didn't care. Or some evenings I wouldn't make it to my room. I'd wake up on the sofa, my backpack still strapped to my arm, my cheek on the arm rest. After a few weeks, I started flushing the pills down the toilet.

"Didn't help at all?" Ben pulled a Spock eyebrow. "What was it like?"

"You never tried anything? To... get better?" Surely he knew what it was like.

"Well, I wouldn't say exactly. No, not like that. Do you remember? How you felt when it was working?"

I did remember, exactly. "It felt," I said, touching my forehead as if to preserve something, as if something might still be at stake. "It felt like the whole world went silent."

Ben seemed to consider that reality for a minute, staring into his coffee.

"That's no good," he said. "That's no good at all. We can't have that."

"So I stopped taking the pills. It wasn't too long after they prescribed them. I couldn't take it. I lost track of time, weeks were flying by. I started flushing them down the toilet—I don't know why. It was kind of an empty gesture. It's not like anybody was checking to see if I was taking them. I stopped complaining about my stomach aches and pretended to be a little happier, and my mom thought the medication was working great. In a way, it was. It taught me not to talk about anything that was wrong with me. Anything really important. That was wrong."

"Yes." Ben nodded.

"Yes?"

"Yes. I'm understanding more and more why I mistook your presentation as a fugue state."

I laughed, short and sudden. "'Presentation' sounds funny. Like I had one of those foldy, science-fair triptychs."

"You know how hard it is to select terminology for..."

"Things nobody else talks about. Or knows exists. Or for which there are approximations that are..."

"...dreadful." Ben half-smiled.

"Yes."

"You're not crazy," he said, shaking his head slightly.

"Was that a question?"

"No, I'm telling you. I'm certain you already know. But for what it's worth, I can verify it. The craziest thing about you is that you're not crazy." I felt like someone else had said that to me before.

"Does that word even mean anything anymore?"

Ben looked around the coffee shop. "Crazy? Oh yes, it does. Misapplication may dull a word in broad contexts. But where it counts," he tapped the edge of his coffee cup with his fingers, "it means a lot."

About the third or fourth time Ben and I met for coffee, things got real, as they say. Right off, he asked me what bothered me the most about the visitations.

"I don't know. These ones recently, the ones where time is missing—that strikes me as a problem, I have to say. Before that, I think it was the... loneliness. Isolation. It was happening to me all the time, but I never told anybody, so all of those stories were just getting trapped there. They weren't getting told still, not to anybody but me. And every single one of them—"

I stopped short, because I hadn't thought of it before, what I had been storing up. They all seemed to have big ranges of emotion, from deep sorrow to fear to joy to pride—but there was one emotion all of them shared.

"Every single one of them is a knot of unfulfilled desire. Desire to move, like irresistible planetary rotation. I think it's what makes me want to lie down on the ground so often when it happens. Like I need to feel something physically stronger, and the only thing handy is gravity." *Was that right?* It seemed right, and so I nodded at my own statement.

"That," Ben said, pointing at the top of my head. To some particular region of my brain, I'm sure. "That is why it feels like a fugue state. Tell me, besides the missing time, what specifically is worrying you now? Do certain stories haunt you, for instance? Haunt—poor choice of words, maybe."

"No, no. 'Haunt' is right, denotative and connotative. Sometimes. Really poignant emotions, like disappointment, loss. The stories of children. Because those often feel like the teller doesn't understand what happened him or herself. Not that they want to tell me, that they want me to be a record or a conduit, like usual. The ones who seem to want me to explain what happened. Those haunt me, yes." The picture. I thought about the girl in the picture.

He looked directly at me. "Do you want to be haunted?"

"No. No, I don't."

There was a long pause. Ben drank the last of his coffee and stood up. He said, "Then the real question is what you're going to do about that, and when." And then he walked away.

Or I think he walked away. I looked up, and he was gone.

CHAPTER TWENTY TWO

NORA AND I WERE huddled around the light box, looking at slides and negatives. We return to the tactile—digital's great, convenient and cost-efficient, but Nora likes the weight of film, the depth.

"Show me the picture again. Yeah, okay. Now look at the one I took of you." Nora recreated the picture of Justine with me playing her. I never did feel like I got the stance right, but Nora was right about the facial expression. It was almost identical, a defiant squint, lips almost pursed as if she was caught at the beginning of saying the word "You!" to the photographer.

"Yeah," Nora said with some satisfaction. "I think we got it. Don't you?"

Cause and effect is a tricky system. I'm a door trying to be a window, remember? The problem was that I didn't remember. I thought being a window would make everything better.

It would have been ungrateful and shortsighted to say so, but Nora and I were a little disappointed going through the Crybaby Lane pictures to find absolutely zero unexplained phenomena. No mysterious fog, no blurry figures. No luminous orbs. What Nora did have were stunning photos of young women dancing like electric trapezoids, the eerie and luminous results of her experiments with shutter speed. Light banners streaming off of their bodies shattered in jagged furls across the empty field under the stars. The first batch of prints was spread out on the kitchen table; another was pinned to the strings we put up in the tiny dark room/closet, drying.

"These are really lovely. Spooky. But consoling, too."

"Yeah," Nora said brightly, but a little wistfully. "The tree looks nice in this one."

"Oh, absolutely." I bent closer to the one she held up, a silhouette of bursting branches. "Like nerve endings against the sky."

We had looked at the digital ones. Nora had shot both film and digital on the tiny screen that night, but the old school film ones felt different.

My phone started making its typewriter noise. It was a text from Thomas.

Where'd you go?

I texted back a question mark and an emoji of a taco, which seemed about right for answering a random question.

"Ms. Galloway thinks I should send these two to the PTSA Reflections contest." In one, K and D were outstretched like starfish reaching toward each other. It was impossible to tell whether they were just coming together or beginning to separate. Nora had enhanced the contrast and saturated the color; their faces were blurred and their hair spread out in points. The photo seemed to spill over with energy and activity, but without narrative—lyric and eternal, an electric Grecian urn. In the other, the car headlights were shining through the low grass. My foot and lower leg appeared in one beam, my scuffed, ancient cowboy boot and ragged jeans. Above the knee, though, I was shadowed out, outside the light beam.

The typewriter noise again.

Hello? I came to pick you up, and they said you left already.

"I had to mess with the settings a little to get that one. Slow down the shutter speed. That was one from the series I took from the tripod."

"Slow down the shutter speed," I repeated. I sent an emoji of a frog while I tried to figure out what I was missing.

There was this one photo—even with just its one foot of a human form, this one had a narrative. I pointed and nudged Nora.

"Remember this one? You showed it to me on the screen when you took it—"

"Right, and you said it was your favorite one. Weirdo."

Click clack text. *WTF does that mean—you hopped off? You frog-got? See you at home.*

I did like it. I liked it because it looked like something was just about to happen. *What's that fancy word?* Synecdoche, the piece announcing the whole. This picture was about what you don't see but you know is there. The story that was in the dark, in the part of the world our awareness doesn't reach. It was just my foot, but it felt like a portrait. There I was, that piece of me in the present, the rest of me in the shadows, looking for the stories, the dark boundaries. I had gotten comfortable there in those margins.

It seemed like I belonged there. That's my land, where I grew up. No-man's-land. I don't know how to step out of it.

I started to text a sad face, then deleted it. I was looking for the Munch *Scream* emoji. Nora sat at the computer, cropping and brightening another photo of me as Justine.

"Something's still not exactly right, but I think I can fix it."

But I don't know if she can. I've asked her to help me eclipse myself, I realize. I start to imagine how to apologize for that, but instead I remember that night with Nora and her friends, how we decided we were hungry and ended up at the new Waffle House over in Mission Valley. Since it was a Waffle House next to a record store where bands play, just barely off the campus of a giant university, the whole place was strikingly and comically busy at one o'clock in the morning. Mostly comical because the girls were so struck by how busy it was. The brittle music of utensils against each other, dishes and cups ringing like bells, and the continuous chatter—fluorescent as the lights—that broke the darkness outside into pieces. You know how Anglo Saxons thought of life as a moment of brightness against the eternal dark, a sparrow flying through the windows of a bustling mead hall at night? The equivalent philosophy for a Southerner would be a crow bird flying through a Waffle House at night.

"What are all these people doing in here? Who eats at this hour?" K with the questions, of course.

"We are." Nora gets cranky when her blood sugar is low.

"All these people could not possibly have been out looking for ghosts." D is sweet, but I find it hard to tell when she's being ironic. Are teens ironic only when they are not ironic? How can anyone be simultaneously naïve and ironic? I've become very old.

"No, most of them are out looking for beer." K's the one I'll have to help bail out one fine day.

"Looks like a lot of them found it."

"And one another." Nora scowls at a couple in a booth, pawing each other with syrup-sticky hands, no doubt. She needs a waffle, stat, before she bites somebody.

"Oh, look; four boys with hairdos. Somebody's gig is over." I like playing Spot the Band. It's a skill I can teach these young women.

"One of them is asleep on a waffle," D observes, affection in her tone.

"That would be the drummer." Well. It would be.

"Is it too weird if I get a waffle with my grilled cheese?" K fans herself with the plastic menu while Nora cranes around looking for a waitress. She answers with her head turned.

"Everything comes with a waffle. A waffle comes with a side of waffle."

"A subwaffle."

"Indeed."

I can't help noticing the young men at the next table noticing my troop of young ladies. Just in case I hadn't, or they hadn't, the young men began to talk loudly enough for us to hear them. Their sports talk was the wrong way to impress the girls. I could have told them that, but it wouldn't have helped. It was too late for them when they believed that Axe commercial, much less left the house in those shoes. They were irritating me mostly at this point because I'd gotten interested in eavesdropping on a different conversation over at the counter between two very serious-faced hipster boys whose body language suggested actual defeat of some kind, and not just ironic distance.

"Dude, is there even a movie out called *Birdman*? I don't think I've heard of one."

"Evidently. I mean, yeah. I think I've heard of it. It's got Kevin Costner in it or something."

I turned around and jumped in, because for once I knew what was happening, and the people I was hearing were alive and in the room with me.

"Oh yeah—it's a real movie. It's Michael Keaton. Based on a Raymond Carver story, I think." Confirmation. I felt like Google must feel, if Google were a real person and had feelings.

"That's right—now I remember. I get those two confused, Michael Keaton and Kevin Costner. They look just alike."

Old, I thought, is what they look like to you, but that's okay. The other one seemed to know who Raymond Carver was.

"Like that movie *Short Cuts*. Okay, it kinda makes sense now." They turned back to each other in deep consideration.

"Yeah, she's like, a lit major or something. I mean, she's pretty cool."

"Sure she is. That's why he probably got mixed up. I mean, the fact that it was even within reason that it might have been what she meant, you know. He was pretty fucking stoked."

"And Redman is in town. With Method Man."

"Yeah. It's totally understandable. How it happened. He was like, 'Sweet, I'll get tickets,' and she was like, 'Sweet,' and then..."

It became clear, following the trajectory of the conversation, that these guys had come from the Method Man &

Redman show at the Lincoln Theater. Their tickets had
been provided by an absent friend, who had purchased the
tickets to take his girlfriend—mistaking her request to go
see *Birdman,* the film based on Raymond Carver works, on
Friday night, for a request to see hip hop icons Method
Man & Redman. With some fairly serious consequences,
based on the debriefing going on. The aforementioned
girlfriend, it seemed, was an advocate of neither hip hop
nor pot legalization, for which the Method Man & Redman
tour was raising awareness. But not too heightened an
awareness. A low-key, chill kind of awareness. Not tweaky-
paranoid awareness.

"No way, man. Buuurrnnnn."

"Man. Redman AND Method Man."

That's a lot of men, I thought to myself. Wrong man,
third man, no man left behind. There were a lot of jokes to
be made, but they were hipsters who had suddenly become
post-ironic, so it was a serious situation. It was fascinating.
Scary, a little. They were almost... sweet. But with trucker
hats.

"I know, man. I hear you."

"That's like, dude. Not happening all the time."

"I know."

"I mean, I would have said to her, Babe, it's Method
Man & Redman, and I don't know when or if I'd be able to
see them again, it's like a maybe like a one-time thing."

"Right. Well, he may have told her that. Maybe he did?"

"No, man. It went down like this. He got home and she
was dressed to go, and she was like, 'what time is the show?'
and he was like 'Doors at eight, but they won't start until

nine at least, but everybody's going early to get high in the parking lot.' And she was like, 'What the holy fuck.'"

"Oh, shit."

"When he gave me the tickets, he just said, Man, I gotta let it go. I ain't getting this worked out in time to see this thing happen. You go for me."

"Harsh. Yeah. I don't know why he didn't even, like, try to convince her. I'd have at least tried, you know. Make her be the one to say she didn't want to go, you know."

They sat there for a minute in silence, drinking sodas out of the big red plastic Waffle House tumblers. Everything in Waffle House is so tactile, the bumpy plate edges, the pebbled plastic drink cups, the fat, satisfying rims of the coffee mugs. I ran my finger along the edge of mine. K was across from me dissecting her hash browns. D was holding her drink in the air, gaping at the bottom of the cup for some reason. And Nora was drinking a tiny coffee creamer by sucking its insides out through a coffee stirrer.

"*What?*" She looked at me defensively while poking the stirrer through another creamer lid and sucking up another.

How do we ever find each other in this world? Those boys were only a few years older than the girls here. Closer in age to them than I am to Thomas, I thought. Thomas would often remark "I was four years old," as I talked about the year when I was too young to get into the Pier and I stood in the underground of Cameron Village to listen to the dB's. Or the year I got married the first time ("I was eleven"). It didn't seem like anything now, of course. Thank goodness we didn't meet then, though. Could I ever have seen him as not-eleven?

"Dude, here's the thing. Method Man & Redman may be like, an individual once-in-a-lifetime thing. But finding a good girlfriend—a real one, an understanding one—that's not even a once-in-everybody's lifetime thing."

His friend nodded. "She's really smart. And she's pretty, too. And she talks to us, too, man. Like we are real people."

"Man, if she really had liked Method Man, I'm pretty sure she'd be too good for him."

"Good point, man. Good point. I mean, we know he doesn't listen."

"Yeah, we all learned that here, I think."

They ruminated for a moment on the novelty of that knowledge.

"I kinda want to see that movie now, though. You know what I mean?"

"Oh, no doubt. Wanna go tomorrow?"

"Dude, I gotta work."

"Whatever, dude. Life is short."

I snatched a couple of bites from Nora's chocolate chip waffle while she kept on draining tiny cups of creamer. I looked around the table at the girls.

"Hey." They looked up, their straws and forks and French fries dangling from their fingers, their eyes bleary but shining at the excitement of being out in the dominion of adults, at least in some vaudeville version of it. Eating things in public in the middle of the night. We do stuff like this.

"Try not to be too good for other people."

K and D glanced sidelong at each other. Nora's creamer cup rattled out a death-sigh.

"Okay?"

They all muttered confused assents. I picked up all the checks and told them to meet me at the door. You have to give people a chance to do right by you. You have to open the avenue for generosity. What can anything in this world ever give you if your heart won't open to accept it? How can anyone or anything even know you're there, if you hide your desires, put away your strength and your passion in the shadows? Self-sufficiency is admirable and all, but we're pack creatures when it comes right down to it. We need to rest in the comfort of our species, close up to the fire on the cold, dark nights. Not just on the cold, dark nights—not just when the predators come. In our moments of great perfection and joy, too. Without witnesses, our joy means nothing. When we share what we love, hey, that's when we lift up everybody.

Clickety Clack. Typewriter. I forgot to hit "send." Where did these words come from? From me?

CHAPTER TWENTY THREE

IT WAS ONE OF THOSE mornings. You know which. One of those. And I was being managed, and it was making things a *lot* worse on this particular occasion.

"You *know* how much I can't stand feeling like I've forgotten something." Pretending he's listening, Thomas smiles at me sympathetically, but still takes my hand to walk me out the door, ignoring my protests.

"Look at me. Eyeballs." He says "eyeballs" to Edgar when he's trying to get him to listen to a particular point. So yes, I am being talked to like a four-year-old. I'm having Edgar-level focus issues. Or Edgar has inherited his focus issues from me. Or he's just four. And some days I am four, too. I worry about all of these things simultaneously. "You haven't forgotten anything. You told me to remind you of that. It's phantom-limb syndrome in your brain."

Even though I was in a state, I knew I wasn't myself and that Thomas was right. I had explicitly told him he would need to remind me that the sense of impending failure and distress was not my own. This feeling had been building throughout November, and from the beginning, I knew it wasn't mine. But I couldn't place the source. I didn't remember where I was when I first felt it—if it had been location-based, like most of my narratives, it would have been easier to compartmentalize. But it had come along with me at some point.

"It's not even pressure to meet a deadline. It's like a I know a deadline is coming that I have already not met."

Thomas considered my statement, organizing it in his mind into something more linear, I could see. "Leave it to you," he said, "to redefine space and time to expand the possible available intervals for anxiety. Are you telling me you have ghost anxiety?"

I answered frostily, "When you put it that way, it sounds very *silly*."

"That's not what I meant to do. Value judgments won't really be helpful, anyway. And silly or not, it sounds like a difficult problem to resolve. On your terms, I mean. Most of your worst tangles with the other side have at least had some kind of tangible footprint in this world."

That was true. While I had realized that the place-ment of Granny's ashes was more symbolic than causal, I had been able to relieve some of the immediate pressure by finding a place for them that was more final than my bookshelf. Even little everyday intrusions often required me to address the source. Most times acknowledgement was enough. But I couldn't see where this one was coming from. Someone seemed to want me to do *something*. Deep passion with no direction can be scary. I was a little scared. I tried to keep listening without freezing up completely, waiting for the incomplete message. I tried to remember my dreams. *Whatever you are,* I said every night, *leave me a message, or leave me alone, because I'm really busy, and unless you give me some more information, you're just making it hard on both of us.*

Thomas reached for reality and asked, "What's your plan for the afternoon?"

"I'm picking up Nora from school, and we're going over to the dark room to pick up her photos for the contest. I'll probably get coffee with Ben before."

"How is he? I'd still like to meet him sometime."
Thomas had taken a liking to Ben, my seeming ally in
the realm of the rational, even with his own experience
of the irrational. Like me, Ben's transparency apparently outweighed his eccentricity for Thomas, who valued
transparency above all virtues. It was the way I had uncon-
sciously maintained my status with him all these years.
That, and my deviled eggs. "You should tell him. Well, I
guess he'll know." Thomas had gotten used to Ben's immediate apprehensions of my mental state. Their mysterious
friendship, despite never meeting in person, developed
out of Thomas's own perpetual transparency. It was kind of
a relief not to have to explain anything, I guess. Or maybe
that's how friendships are these days. In absentia. Low risk.

I had tried writing about the sense of dread, the
downward spiral that seemed to be happening. I figured
putting some language around it might help me see its
outline. So far, nothing was helping. That's what Ben and
I were talking about that day, waiting in line, the barista
looking up once in awhile in a curious fashion.

"Maybe it's just a really strong bout of existential
awareness," I offered, while Ben ordered a quad latte in
a twelve-ounce cup. He also shared my relative immunity
to caffeine. No amount seemed to be enough when my
antennae were in overdrive, like now.

He craned his neck, tipping his chin upward. "That's
not what I'm getting. Are you really sure you haven't
forgotten anything? Not to make it worse, but there's a
true sense of loss, a missing piece. I'm sorry to ask, but is it
the anniversary of something traumatic? Maybe something
you don't even think about often?"

"No, spring is usually the bad time for all of that. May,

sometimes August. This time of year is my happiest, since I was a kid. The leaves start falling and I'm good until Easter."

"Something definitely wants to be completed. It feels very personal, too. Something coming into being. An entity."

"It's getting a little *Rosemary's Baby* in here," I chuckled, but failed to put Ben off the scent. He was like that once he got going.

"No, no. It's something meaningful. I'd say to you, but knowing how you are able to adopt the emotional pasts of other people..."

"I'm haunted. By someone else's failure. That's about the lamest thing I've ever contemplated."

"I don't know if it's good or bad news, but it seems to me like it's unfolding itself for you. You're only meant to watch it. You can't change it. Only see it. Tell about it, maybe. If you can."

There it was, the tiny potential failure for me—there was something to tell, and the only way I could tell it was to catch it like a big, stubborn butterfly. It was my story now. I had to pry it loose from its origin, but it had become a part of me, and now it wouldn't be just my job to tell it, I had to live with it, too.

I'd get to tell it when I netted it. When I pinned it down. Like the fancy bug it was.

Chapter Twenty Four

Of all things, I had a voice message from my old friend Francis. It had been a long while since we had talked. We hadn't seen one another for a while, and hadn't chatted since his virtual presence at the unusual interment of Granny's ashes in the library foundation.

"I've been thinking about you. Let's chat. Call me when you have a minute. Do not call from the car; I heard about your chakra shenanigans. What are you doing with your life, lady?"

His reference to "chakra" made me realize he'd talked to Thomas. The worry was catching. I decided to ruminate on that a bit before calling him back. I could text him. I typed, *I miss you, Francis.* I typed, *Sorry.*

It was a valid question he was asking. What *am* I doing with my life? This was not the plan. The truth is, a year ago I wouldn't have set foot on this haunted land. For most of my life I'd have told you it was the gateway to doom. Little-girl me sat out there in that tobacco field with a transistor radio to my ear singing along to the Clash like it was a prayer to get my ass out of there. Should I Stay or Should I Go, go, go, as fast as humanly possible. I swore I would never drive down this road again if I could just be smart enough to make good grades and go to college and escape.

But it all just seemed to happen like magic. The call from Charlotte that started it all, this chain of events back to buying the land—that was only part of it. Buying the land led to reconciliation, the recovery of my cousins I had missed for so many years, who I avoided so I could avoid my father. And Christopher, who had become so much a part of my life. Not just busting down doors, either. We'd had to go over all of this, the two of us, since he grew up on the same land but at a different time, with a different mother. We had to sift through the horrors of the attic, the real one and the imaginary ones, and we could do that together now. It was helping. But the same violence and the same call to the woods, the hiding place. The voices that could erase your world. But whose origins hid away, too. I know they say the Devil you know is a better Devil than the one you don't. But that's not how we grew up. Both of us spent a long time looking for new devils.

There's no parking in front of the State Archives Building in downtown Raleigh, but there is a place you can tie up your horse. If you've got a sticker there's a side lot. We don't have a sticker, me and Ben. It was Ben this time, not Francis, not Thomas, who I had trusted to help me unravel this trouble, some kind of trouble I could no longer locate, not in this world, not in a past world, not on Nora's Poodle Planet. Not even in an uncertain calendar unfolding on land haunted by something. Something human? Or not. If I brought it myself—if my own desire to get away from the father I hated had built this narrative—if my wishes, good or bad, had determined this outcome, I needed to know all of that now. I'd brought a lot of people with me into this story, and I had to know where it was coming from. *And it seemed to me to be coming from the land itself.*

I was studying the parking lot list of rules and regula-tions when I heard the gravel crunch and saw a garish orange Mercedes Benz roll into a handicapped space. Ben got out with great care, shaking some ashes off his lap. Maybe this hadn't been a good idea. Also, I was pretty sure I'd never seen him drive before.

"Is that your car?"

I don't know what kind of answer would have been consoling.

"Loaner," Ben growled. He flapped the folds of his coat as if he still needed to loosen debris from the folds.

"The Jesus fish is a nice touch."

"What?" Ben crouched around the corner of the bumper to peer more closely. "Oh. Yes. Actually it has tiny feet on it and says 'Nietzsche.'"

"You mean 'Darwin'? The fish with feet say 'Darwin.'"

"You name your fish; I'll name mine. Besides, one of these fishy appendages is holding a gun."

I noticed his right taillight was busted up pretty badly and the fender drooped a little. He saw me eying it and shrugged.

"Come on," he said. "We've got a long day's work. Let's head inside."

Ben explained that he'd already come last week to scout out some of the records we'd need. "There's not much, but I think I may have found some mention of your great-grandfather's land purchase in tax records. There was some possibly relevant material in a couple of local church histories," Ben's attention to detail could be a nerve-wracking distraction at times, but today it was essential.

Ben's shadow blocked the reflection of the street in the glass doors. He pushed the silver handle and held the door open for me, his coat like a curtain. Inside, behind a desk that might have been there since 1962, a woman with a brunette Raleigh bob haircut gave the barest of nods to us, and we continued to the documents room.

You notice the maps on the wall first. Maps of all kinds, enormous ones, some over two hundred years old. Delicately shaded and lettered. Do you know, you can color any map using only four colors and never have two adjacent regions the same tone. Doesn't matter how many regions, either. Four colors is all you need.

"That theory isn't proven irrefutably," Ben reminded me. We had to whisper. Not because anyone told us to, but because when you're in awe, that's what you do.

"Give this to that fellow over there at the counter, and I'll put our coats and bags in the lockers."

I took the slip of paper Ben gave me over to a freckled man in suspenders. He disappeared behind a wooden swinging door with a window like a porthole. Ben stood by me and offered a pencil from a handful of freshly-sharpened Ticonderogas.

"No pens—but you know that," he reminded me.

"No snacks in your pockets."

The man in suspenders placed two boxes on the counter.

"That's right," he said. "And you can only take one of these in at a time. You'll find magnifying glasses inside, on the tables. And I know I don't have to tell you—no phones, no cameras."

"No photos."

"Absolutely no photos." Suspenders man had a dimple on one side when he smiled. "But if you really need a scan of something, I'll see what I can do."

The first box was already resting on the work table;

we slid the cloth cover off and each pulled out a folder. Deeds, mostly, and the reading was dry.

"'Mr. J. S. Birdwell lived in the second house east of Green's Chapel, later owned and occupied by the Sauls family. Thalia Sauls states that her family bought the house from Mr. Birdwell, and that the date '1898' is carved on the porch.'"

"I remember the Birdwell farm. That's one road over. But it's getting close. Some of the Sauls folks lived on our road, I think. At one time. In the big house with the guinea hens that used to try to kill me when I first started driving."

Ben looked over his spectacles at me. "Your poultry issues? Do they predate—"

"I see where you're going. No, I hated chickens way before I could drive." That house was gone. One of the first things I noticed when I came back to Camden Road was that the Birdwell house had burned to the ground, it seemed. There were still steps, but that was about it. I made a mental note to check later for the '1898'—would it be a confirmation of sorts to find it? What kind of confirmation?

The afternoon wore on, more sets of boxes. Church records. An anecdotal history written by a Garner First Baptist Church deacon in the 1940s, with an epigraph from Hebrews. "'These all died in faith, not having received the promises, but having seen them afar off, and were persuaded of them, and embraced them...'"

This time Ben did not look at me, just sat back and continued to recite to the end of the verse while staring into his empty hands: "'...and confessed that they were strangers and pilgrims on the earth.'"

At the word "stranger," I looked up to see if suspenders man was watching us. Promises far off. I wanted to be persuaded. I wanted to be familiar, to see my reflection in something.

It was late in the day before it came. "I think I found something," I started slowly, not certain. "I always knew my great-grandfather bought his farmland from a bigger plantation. The old house aunt Lucinda lives in—it dates to the turn of the century. But the fireplace and the chimney are from before the war, another house. I mean, kind of the same house, but all the parts replaced.

"What happened to the first one?"

"Oh, who knows—the same things that happened to every house down old family roads in North Carolina. Yankees burned it, termites ate it, somebody fell asleep and a kerosene heater turned over... I'm pretty sure this name here," I pushed the manuscript closer to Ben, "this name. Urias. That's the family name of the people he bought it from. The Camdens have a lot of the Urias plantation land, but my great-grandparents had a small piece of it. They didn't move there until the 1920s, though."

I thought about Edgar. When we were at Lucinda's house, at the Crooked Man's grave. The Crooked Man. When we were kids, we learned that he had been a disabled child of the Urias family. We thought maybe that's why he wasn't buried up in Mt. Moriah Cemetery with everybody else. Maybe since he had never left home, his mother wanted to keep him close.

"The Crooked Man?"

"We kids called him that. He walked funny. But we thought it was because—"

"You thought he was a monster. A horror movie character."

"Well. He wasn't real. So it was scary."

"No, he was real. *That's* why he was scary." Despite what great-granddaddy said about him not hurting us. I could remember great-grandaddy's face close, the smell of butterscotch. *He ain't gone hurt nobody.*

"Then there were the little people in the attic. We used to hoist each other up to look in there."

Ben sighed and looked back at the record I had set in front of him. "Why on earth would you want to do such a thing. Little people. Is that what you called them, then?"

"I was really more scared of them than I was the Crooked Man. Josie and I. We... we were..." Caroline was holding me up that time. I screamed when I saw them. Whatever they were. The idea that they were up there in the attic, all the time, busy doing whatever it was they were doing. The Crooked Man just stood there on the landing, sad as hell. *He ain't gone hurt nobody.* But nobody said the Little People wouldn't hurt nobody.

"Well, let's not get sidetracked by your childhood traumas. We could be here for weeks." Ben seemed to be losing patience faster than usual today. Or maybe too much focus on the past had me jumpy myself. "So if I am to glean anything of use from the transaction earlier, coupled with the grammatical stew here that suffices for a local account of familial association, one might reasonably conclude that this homeplace of yours is a chunk that fell off of a plantation connected to local luminary, William Polk. At the very least, it was at one time a cotton plantation operated by one John B. Johns. Miss Scarlett, we have a Tara for you. Or maybe a little piece of the letter R in 'Tara.'"

"It says here that when Sherman's troops were coming, Mrs. Johns hid part of the livestock down in the woods. She sent a servant to hide them. She also had slop jars placed on the stairs to the attic and hid her valuables in there. With the winter hams."

"Ah yes. Preserve the pork products. A plucky Southern belle she must have been. 'As God is my witness, I'll never lack hocks again!' If she was so brave, why didn't she fill those Yankee behinds with lead and send them back to Hell?"

I tried to explain how the whole story probably came out of this family's personal lore, probably not even real. Lots of people tell stories like these. The point was to highlight her hostessing abilities—she charmed the terrible Sherman, fed his men, protected her home and didn't give away the farm. But Ben wasn't having any of it.

"Kill the Yankee! Kill the Yankee!" he kept singing. I swatted at him with an index card.

"Look, calm down. Suspenders man is going to come in here and get us."

"What kind of Southern girl are you? Sticking up for that Satanic Sherman? You're getting more than a white glove penalty for this, young'un." He started swinging his arms and marching in place.

"You know as well as I do that Sherman was a genius." Now I was off topic and distracted. If I have a truly fatal flaw, it's needless precision. "He was the only one who understood how the fighting contingent of the Confederacy had been buffaloed by the rich men who sent them to fight for a lifestyle that didn't even benefit them. All that flower of Southern Womanhood crap. Those soldiers were fighting for people who wouldn't have sat on the same pew with them in church, but they'd have fought until every one of them was dead. All for the image of honor. Sherman saved more Southern lives than any Southern general."

Ben stopped his little dance and tilted his head to the side. Then he gave me the finger.

"All right. That's enough. I've had enough of you today."

Ben followed me as I gathered the materials back into their tidy folders and returned them to their cloth box. He pretended to pick imaginary bugs off of my clothing, and I brushed him away once or twice but mostly I just ignored him.

"Honestly. Why are you being such a *dick* today? You have to understand the way people here tell stories. If everybody that had claimed to see Robert E. Lee riding home after Appomattox had actually seen the man, he would have had to have taken two years to ride home in a route composed of figure eights. Everybody who saw a white horse in the distance for the next decade thought they saw Lee." Ben had put on a pair of sunglasses—I suppose he had them in his pocket? We still didn't have our coats or bags back. Anyway, I couldn't tell where he was looking.

"Didn't your family tell stories?" I finally asked him.

His face didn't change. "My family," he said carefully, "had no stories whatsoever."

Ben pealed off in his hideous orange Mercedes without

a goodbye. What I didn't tell Thomas or Ben or anybody that day, because I was still trying to pace it out in my head, was that the Johns cotton plantation's numerous slaves had lived in a piece of bottomland described in detail in the family historical documents. The descriptions of the terrain, the detail that the piece of bottomland flooded out regularly, even the grove of trees and the rock creek that had been my playground, the rocks my cousins and I crawled around on that may have been Indian land we thought: all of it had been the site of the Johns slave quarters.

Now we live here on this bottomland. I watch Thomas's headlights come over the crest of the hill and glide down the driveway at dusk, and I smile. But when I was a little girl and saw headlights coming, I'd run and shut off the lamp in my room, shut the door and try to lock it. Hide my head under the covers before my father's heels clattered on the slate porch. Most nights he'd ignore me. But sometimes he'd open the door and watch me. Sleeping, he thought. And I'd wish for him to die before he took one step toward me.

Tonight I'm waiting for Thomas's headlights. Deep in my pocket, my fingers find the slip of paper from this morning, the paper Ben gave me for the archivist with the snazzy suspenders. In the dark, here at home, it just looks like random numbers and symbols. But there's this one word "Bethel," and I remind myself to ask Thomas why it seems familiar. If I can stay awake until he gets home.

CHAPTER TWENTY FIVE

WE'D BEEN ON THE LAND for *months*. The house was well underway; we figured by spring we'd be moving in. I felt confident I'd get a handle on the insomnia and the slightly unsettling time lapses by then. In a way, I felt pretty confident that the house itself would put a rest to all that. That by making our own place out here, we'd finally ease into a balance with the history of this place. A history that had no written record, except for about two hundred years of land deeds. Nothing about anything ever happening here. Most of history is just that anonymous, you know. The good parts and the bad parts. You negotiate that space every day. You just don't always know when it's happening.

"You've been pacing again." It's three o'clock or so in the morning. I already know that, but Thomas is checking his phone when I try to creep back into our room.

"I'm sorry I woke you up. I can't sleep."

"No, definitely not walking around like that, you can't. What's bothering you? Another dream?"

"It's too cold to pace outside. Plus, critters."

"The critters are asleep."

"No, no. Not everything out here sleeps."

There was some rustling, then, "What are you people doing?" Nora stood in the doorway to our room.

"Not sleeping." Thomas yawned, and I apologized.

"Waking you up. Sorry. Tiny house problems."

"I was already not sleeping." Nora jumped onto the end

of the bed, curled up like a comma.

"Well. I guess we could make a short, blunt, human pyramid," I offered.

"Ha! Guildenstern. We just read that for English." Nora was pleased to make the connection, and I reveled in a moment of having a child who gets Tom Stoppard references. At 3 a.m.

"Whatever we do, let's not end it being pursued by a bear. Or any woodland creatures. I don't think we've got any bear out here," Thomas warned.

"We've already had it out with the neighborhood vampire pig." Ever since the night of the campout/ shootout/barbecue, Nora liked to pretend we had a vampire pig infestation in the woods. I did not enjoy this fantasy.

We all started laughing. "Don't wake up Edgar," I warned. "That was some pretty good barbecue."

"I know. Wait here," Nora trotted off, and Thomas propped up pillows. I was already sitting Indian-style on the bed. Nora came in and jumped up into the middle with a pack of playing cards in her hand.

"The only thing I know how to play is Solitaire," she announced.

"Don't tell me you brought a pack of cards in here at 3 a.m. so that we could watch you play Solitaire."

"No! Well, but what can we play? Teach me something. How do you play War?"

"Well, you split the deck like this, and then each player deals out a card... but see, that's a two-person game."

Thomas shuffled the pack.

"Oh, we can play Gin or Crazy Eights. They're both good for three people." One thing I did know was cards.

"I'm not sure I remember all the rules to either of those. But we do have this thing called The Google." Thomas was already consulting his phone.

"Yes. I remember most of how to play Gin, except for some of the scoring. And I remember Crazy Eights. We played cards all the time. I used to kick everybody's ass at Gin in college. I played the waiters in my dad's restaurant. I played my dad. Of course, he'd tear up the cards if he lost, so that was really more terrifying than diverting, as a card game really should be."

"Yes. Well, I think I can remember Crazy Eights. How many cards?" Thomas put the phone down and looked at me for directions.

"We each get seven, then you turn the first card face up to start the discard pile."

"Okay, I'll shuffle; you cut."

"I've always wanted to learn how to play bridge," Nora ventured.

"Yeah, we need four people for that."

"I know. I bet we could make that happen. Edgar's not old enough." I was trying to calculate how many years that would take.

"Maybe Mimi would play with us."

"Well, she knows how. Man, people who play bridge, it's like golf. They get really into it." I used to make the snacks for Mom's bridge group. Lots of Easy Cheese and Chicken in a Biscuit crackers.

"I like cards. It seems so much more congenial than chess. And less pretentious." Nora will walk a mile to avoid a snob.

"Yeah. 'Why not come over for some bridge?' sounds like snacks and alcohol might be involved."

"But 'Hey, come over and let's play chess!'"

"A gateway to *Dungeons and Dragons*," Thomas eyed us both, "...and *Monty Python's Flying Circus*."

"Oh hey. It's not that bad."

"Either that or 'And after, we'll take practice SATs.'"

"Ugh. Okay, yeah." Nora was semi-proud of being a semi-nerd.

"Okay, everybody got seven? You start, Nora. It's the six of clubs, so put down a club or a six."

"Six of hearts. I've got a three of hearts. Nic?"

"Got it. Three of diamonds."

"Great. Okay, Nora."

Nora put down a two of diamonds.

"Aha. Now you take two." I pointed at Thomas.

"What?" Thomas looked up. Nora glanced back and forth between us. "What are you talking about?"

"She played a two; you have to take two."

"Well, I played a three, and you didn't take three."

"That's because you only take cards when it's a two, and then you take two. Unless you can't play, then you take cards until you can play." I was going to have to explain the rules for a few hands until they got it.

"I can play—I don't need to take any cards."

"Except you have to take two because she played two."

"That is not a rule! You are on the sauce." Thomas kept laughing, and I kept insisting that I had always played this way.

"Look it up, Mr. Google. I'm telling you, it's a rule."

"Horse. Shit. I'm looking. Okay, nothing on the Bicycle site on your Take-2 corollary."

"Try another." I'd been playing Crazy Eights all my life. I knew the freaking rules.

"That's right. Why trust the people who make the cards?" Nora was on her back laughing with her arms and legs waving in the air like a cockroach, begging us to stop so she could breath.

"Okay, nothing on the Hoyle's site. But hold on, I'm willing to go one more and check Wikipedia, the cemetery of fact. Hang on. Oh wait, wait, ladies and gentlemen— Nora, I want you to know that your mother is trying to baffle us with none other than *Canadian* Crazy Eight rules. That's right; foreign variations—how did you even come up with this?"

"My dad taught me the rules—we always played this way. I cannot even believe I fell for this crap. I mean, looking back, it did seem like the rules just got more and more complicated—"

"Wait, are you telling us there are more cards with special superpowers?" Now Thomas and Nora were both laughing.

"Well, sure. Jacks skip the next player, sevens reverse the rotation, and fours allow you to play an extra card..." I counted off on my fingers.

"You have got to be kidding. Was your dad just making these up randomly whenever he got behind? I almost want to play with these awesome carny rules. It's like playing cards with Shiva." Thomas looked at me with a sort of admiration.

Now I was laughing, too. "Just play, just play the normal way."

"You don't at least want the Canadian rules, eh?"

"No, no. Dammit. My childhood was a lie." I faked indignation. Well, I mean, it was mostly fake. Me and indignation have always been on fairly familiar terms.

"We knew that already. Okay. Where were we? Okay, diamonds. I have a seven. Which will not reverse the progression, so you, Nic."

I played a four of diamonds, all by itself, no extras. Nora was stuck so she drew a couple of cards before playing.

I started chuckling again. "One time my Buffalo relatives came to visit and we all sat around playing Crazy Eights, and when you had to draw a bunch of cards, my aunt Marge would say, 'That's a nice Spanish fan you got there, lady. Let's see your castanets!'"

I could see Aunt Marge, her grey hair in a tight bun, her silver glasses. Her laughter like pots and pans in the kitchen, clattering around us. Her hair coming a little undone from the bun, wisps on her forehead. Fresh pasta hanging in her kitchen and her hair coming a little loose. Very loose. Another woman with a high, gray bun. She has a black fan across part of her face. Her hair is coming apart. Her face in a mirror and her hair coming down. Hurry. Hurry. Oh God. It's never... We're never going to make it. *It's time now. Too late. Everyone will miss it. Has to happen now. Have to finish now. We're behind! Don't you see how much the world needs to see this?*

"I don't sleep, you know." She says something like that, the lady holding the fan, but Pierson, the photographer, doesn't respond. He's busy arranging a stack of cushions at the right slope on which for her to recline, but she's just pacing up and down the studio like a large feral cat. He's afraid of her. She's practicing witchcraft. She's using all of us, you know. Pierson looks at me. No, he looks past me.

"This... this is my joy... my life..." She dances a figure eight—she's not graceful. She's a little out of breath. The fan drops to the floor.

He doesn't think she's really talking to him at all. She's diabolical. He's never seen a woman like this. Of course the money she paid him to photo-graph her was important at first, but now, he'd be afraid to stop doing as she asked, even if she couldn't pay anymore. Thank goodness she didn't seem to know. Such a thing wouldn't occur to her. Money was as alien to her as a thimble to a parrot.

She was crouched on the ground now, crawling toward him. Mother of God. Why had this creature been visited upon him? The first day her husband brought her to the studio, she had been barely more than a pretty young girl. But she sat so straight in her evening gown, her hands perfectly arranged, a nest of violets carefully tucked and pinned at her shoulder. Extraordinary ringlets of hair, fashioned in a manner he'd never seen before. Oddly beautiful, deliberately arranged, it was only at the first flash that he noticed the one thing that would never leave her, not as her beauty began to crumble, not as her sense became increasingly scattered. That expression. She had not worn it into the studio, when she had appeared like a forest creature transformed into a young woman. The flashbulb struck open her eyes, and a wild confidence sprang out, pounced; the young photographer had peeked out of his cover to check his skittish model, only to find a ravening Fury where the little girl had just been. He crouched back under the blanket, wondering if his eyes had exaggerated. But the photographs had shown it to be a fact. Not defiance, no. She wasn't staring back at him, the photographer. She became one with the camera. She was looking into her own soul, into the eye of God. Her gaze was the moment of rapture that Baroque artists attempted to portray. She was the moment of creation.

Even now, crawling across the rugs, her hair completely frazzled, unpinned, loose and pushed away from her face like spits of white flame, shocks of lightning, she searched the room for it, the instant. She looked around everywhere, as if a piece of time could run away and hide from her like a mouse.

"Are you ready for me? Are the props in place?"

"Yes, madame. We may proceed when you wish."

Pierson dreaded her arrivals. He longed to tell her he would not continue their work. But every time, afterwards, when she had long left and he had spent hours alone in the dark room of chemicals, they would emerge, the photographs that left him senseless, bewildered, broken with desire for more.

"What happened?" I asked Nora and Thomas. They were sitting there patiently.

"I don't know, but apparently, it's important, and we're about to miss it," Thomas reported.

I looked down at the Queen of Hearts facing up on the discard pile. There was a flash of light. Nora was holding her camera and smiling.

Chapter Twenty Six

Thomas and Nora seemed to be as excited to see the pictures as I was to show them.

"I know who it is that's been keeping me awake," I told Thomas. It was morning. The sun was just starting to turn everything pale, and we were all wiped out from Insomnia-rules Crazy Eights. To which I had apparently truly brought back the "crazy" last night.

I pulled out the computer and showed Thomas another photograph of the Contessa.

"Whoa. I remember her. Yeah, she is something else," he said. Nora sidled over and peered over Thomas's shoulder.

"Hee hee. She is delightful. What is that in her lap? It looks like a squid."

"I can't tell. It may be; this is certainly not the weirdest photo of her. She had over seven hundred taken. She directed all the lighting, staging—bought the costumes."

"Nice. Look at this one—she's like ten feet tall."

"For some she stood on a box or a ladder—in others, she's lying on the floor. In one, it looks like she's sinking in her ballgown like she's in quicksand."

"Whoa! Look at that. It's like those sharpshooter photos. She's looking at the photographer, but through the mirror. All you can see is the back of her head —"

"...and those eyes. She's got the crazy eye, no doubt."

"So see this one? See the gown? This was her costume

for the ball she attended at the height of her affair with
Napoleon III. She was dressed as the Queen of Hearts."

"Oh, so when we were playing cards last night—"

"...and the Queen of Hearts showed up..."

"I guess, yeah! That must have been her triumphant
moment. Looking at her life story, it seems like it sure
would have been a high point. I'm not sure about the
urgency, though."

"Maybe something she wanted to get done?"

"Seems that way. Huh. I guess I'll keep looking."

"And listening," Nora said.

"Yeah, listening."

That's about when Edgar came around the corner to
look at the computer screen. He'd been pretty committed
to *Star Wars* for most of our conversation, but enough
animated gestures from us and he finally decided to look
in to see what was so interesting. I watched him, to see if
anything would register with him at all. He looked at her
for a bit, then turned away.

"You know that lady, Edgar?" Nora asked him, handing
him a piece of the orange she was eating.

"What lady?"

"That lady on the computer?"

"No lady. That's not a lady." Edgar shook his head.

"What do you mean it's not a lady? It's a picture of
a lady, right? A lady in that picture right there?" Nora
pointed to the Contessa, in the middle of the screen.

"That's the light," Edgar said. That's all he would

say about her. That she was the light. He seemed to be completely confused that we would call her anything else at all.

"Are you still having coffee with Ben today?" Thomas was right. I was supposed to meet Ben in town. I had forgotten.

"Damn. Did I put the time in the calendar?"

"If you leave now you can make it. I know he's a stickler for punctuality."

Was he? "I guess. I mean, I'm sure he can wait for me for a few minutes. It's Saturday."

"Where is it you said he works?"

Where did Ben work? When did I tell Thomas? "I have no idea," I started to say, but Thomas was talking.

"You said he hated to wait, that he'd been like that since high school."

"I didn't say that. And I didn't go to high school with Ben."

"Sure you did. Didn't you? I mean, how do you know him?"

"I met him in the Trader Joe's parking lot, remember?"

Thomas just laughed and wagged a finger at me. "Nic," he said, "sometimes your life is like a *Saturday Night Live* sketch that goes on too long. Or Monty Python. I never understood Monty Python."

I stared at him, not sure what to say.

"Well, whoever he is, then. I'll play along. You better get going," Thomas said, kind of sadly I thought.

CHAPTER TWENTY SEVEN

ONE OF THE CHIEF hurdles we'd have to negotiate if we were going to live out here would be the towering obstacle of Family Dinner. To be fair, the biggest problem I had with *these* family dinners over the years was that my father was likely to be present. Now that he had worn down the patience of every last member of the clan, I could come back to the fold without worrying about somebody trying to run some kind of Hayley Mills Parent Trap bull on me. They all knew better.

So we were spending Thanksgiving on the Old Camden Road for the first time ever. I was cautiously optimistic. I mean, I was as excited as I could be for something without alpacas or ice cream. And who knows? Ice cream was a possibility.

My mom was coming out to the farm for Thanksgiving, too. Since Edgar was born we had hosted Thanksgiving, and so naturally she planned to come here this year. She seemed less concerned about our family history out here than I had been. When I had come to her worried about what she'd think of us moving back out there, she'd just said "you forget I'm the one that got that land from your great-grandaddy. He gave it to me, not your father. Hell, nobody was even talking to them then. I said, Grandaddy, I want to build a house out here next to y'all, and he said, Honey, you can build a house out here anyplace you like. And I said I wanted that spot right on top of the hill. Everybody said 'You can't have that spot; it's right in the middle of the tobacco field.' And he said 'if that's the spot she wants, she can have it.' And that's where I built my house."

He ain't gone hurt nobody.

Caroline's kitchen was the biggest, and her dining room would hold us all, so the main part of Thanksgiving was usually at her house. Everybody would have snacks and drinks at Donna's, then we'd move across the street to Caroline's, then the plan was to walk across the back field to Lucinda's, the old house, the homeplace. If it was warm enough out, we'd eat pie on the porch, drink coffee under the plaid wool blankets and watch the same stars our great grandparents had. If it was too cold, we'd sit in her side room, next to what would always seem like great-granny's kitchen. Little Granny, we still called her. If we all got too drunk, well. We were kind of making it up as we went along anyway. Traditions were still fluid in these years. The old ones were gone, and the mean ones were gone. We were just happy to be in the same place. Even Charlotte was back from Australia; they couldn't come for Christmas this year because Charlotte's charity work was keeping her in another hemisphere. But they were here now, and with all of us in the same room, time seemed irrelevant. We were where we had always been, together.

You could see the stand of oaks around the Crooked Man's grave standing at the sink in Caroline's kitchen.

"Where's Sam?"

"He's watching the game. He's gone go get Aunt Ada in the golf cart and bring her over when it's halftime. Hand me that celery over there, honey. In the sink. Thank you."

"Does Lucinda still make that cake, the caramel one with the pecans around the outside?'

"We wouldn't let her come to dinner if she stopped making that cake."

"Outstanding. I've had dreams about that thing."

"Don't tell anybody, but Josie's been making it for the last two years. Nobody can tell the difference. I'm not even sure Lucinda realizes she's not making it anymore. She forgets a lot of stuff."

As if she knew what I was thinking just then, Caroline put down the knife and hugged me, still holding a big old handful of celery. "I'm just so happy," she said, wiping her eyes. "It's so strange, all of us back here. Crazy."

"Here, have more wine," I said, reaching across the counter over the stuffing croquettes for the bottle.

"It's not the wine, honey. But okay I'll have more," she picked up her glass. "Listen, there is one thing I need to tell you—stop there, that's good—yep, I just need to let you know, cause I know you said your mama is coming..."

The whole time I'm listening to this story, I'm factoring in Mom's propensity for fiction, her ability to recast herself as the heroine of nearly any story. And I'm examining my own feelings about the house, factoring my own ability to cast myself in a minor role in a dark narrative lodged somewhere in that space between Sir Walter Scott and Wilkie Collins. In other words, none of this is fact. But some of this has got the truth in it. Like it's holding it in a pair of tongs.

Like I said, she wasn't nearly as superstitious as the rest of us and she didn't have any trouble visiting us out on the land. Further, she had no qualms about spending Thanksgiving with my dad's entire remaining family, especially since not one of them wanted to have any little bit of a piece of him around anymore.

She'd outlasted the bastard, as far as she was concerned,

and she kind of liked being around to enjoy it. She'd outlasted all the mean ones.

Right after we moved out here, she and I sat at the kitchen counter in the tiny house one morning. She was determined to help me come to terms with the decision to come back home. She thought it ought to belong to me, if I wanted it. And to be fair, I was telling her that it was what I wanted.

"Are you feeling any better about all that stuff you were worried about?"

"About Planet Earth? Mom, I'm not sure I've ever been asked a question with a wider scope. You want to give me some field markers or something? I'll do my best to give you an update."

Mom's practical. That's why she's the one that started a business that supports us all. Anything speculative loses her. Not because she's unnerved. She's just got absolutely zero interest in fantasy. About the only relative uncertainty she enjoys is gambling, and that's only because she actually believes she has a demonstrable edge, a near-calling.

"Well, you know all that about the dreams you were having and the... whatever you call it. Ghosts. On the land."

"The haunted garage? The native American spirit presences? The evil, angry energy? Funny you should ask."

"Look, I know you're not going to be happy unless..."

"I planted a whole field of sage in the upper pasture. I plan to set fire to it in April. *Don't look at me that way; I'm kidding.*"

"Well, I just can't tell anymore. I don't understand it,

but that doesn't mean it's not real. There's a whole lot I
don't understand. For instance, your *father*. I don't understand why I lived with *him* for twenty-five years."

"Oh. I got nothing on that one, either."

"But I sure don't believe your father's evil had a thing to
do with this land. And neither should you. You let that go,
now. Your grandfather beat him every day growing up, and
your grandmother was no kind of mother. He didn't have a
chance."

"See, I'd be more inclined to believe that, oh, some
kind of shifting tectonic plates or a deposit of uranium or,
I don't know, disembodied warrior spirits got him all riled
up. Because I just can't blame Granny. If she sucked as a
parent, something would have to be wrong with me."

Mom raised an eyebrow.

"I'm not saying there's nothing wrong with me.
But assuming there *is* anything wrong with me, it's not
Granny's fault. Just like his problems aren't her fault."

"Well, you had *me* to help you."

"Didn't he have you to help him, too? What was he,
fifteen? When you met?"

Mom had to sit back on that one. "Don't lay that one on
me, missy. He came that way." She took a sip of tea. "So.
What exactly do you think is under the garage?"

"Hell. I don't know. I can't prove anything."

And that's the thing. I couldn't prove anything, really.
The bad dreams I was having out here were the same
dreams I'd had all my life. I had decided once I got out
here, after a few bad nights, I could make them fizzle

away, like the tissue paper flowers I made at Vacation Bible
School that got wet in the rain on the way home. I thought
if I could see the anger, I could drive it out. Call it out
and send it away. Brighten it and crop it like a shadowy,
off-kilter photograph. This was either the truth or a lie so
necessary to my well-being that I had decided to believe it.

"That boy they adopted," Mom said. "Oh, how your
grandmother hated him. Hated him so much your Granny
tried to kill her own mother. Went after her with the
kitchen knife. Nobody ever knew the whole story there, and
I know some bad things happened. But it's all over. It was
all over a long, long time ago. This land didn't do that. A
bunch of people did it."

My people. My family. She married in, but I'm the one
tied to them.

"Mom, I'm curious. When you were a little girl and
skinned your knees, did you always pull off the scabs?"

She wasn't listening. "You remember that letter I wrote
that year. The one I sent to all the sisters. Your Granny
didn't speak to me for weeks. It was a blessed time."

Oh good lord, do I ever remember the letter my
mom wrote to my grandmother's sisters. It was not the
usual newsy Christmas missive. I know it was around the
holidays, though, because we had Christmas cards taped
around the sliding doorway to the patio room, taped
so they hung down diagonally, like the stockings on the
hearth. We used to get so many cards; they went all the
way up one side, all the way along the top of the sliding
door, and down to the floor on the other side. I was
sitting underneath the festive archway of cards when I
read the copy of that letter. I'd gotten hold of it, despite

the fact that it had been meant only for the grown-ups.
It was typed, but it was my mother's words, clear enough.
I was really young, but can remember the little thrill I
felt, seeing such familiar language printed like a book. It
sounded like talking, but it looked like writing. There was
a little profanity, too. Might have been the first time I ever
saw "jackass" or "stuck-up bitch" written down.

"That letter." My mom laughed. "Damn, I was *young*. I
had no idea what was going to come down on me. I thought
I was gonna straighten those old broads out, tell them they
ought to appreciate one another before they were all dead
and in the ground." She started to laugh hard. "I got 'em
talking to each other again, that's for sure. Talking about
how they were gonna kick my ass. I remember Lucinda
calling me up, so mad she was crying, saying 'We all
thought you were such a nice girl!' Well, that's just cause
you didn't know me yet, I told her. Your grandmother and
her sisters. Like five different chapters out of the book of
all kinds of crazy."

I had stopped worrying about having the mental issues
my grandmother and her sisters had. I knew I had some of
their tendencies. But like the missing eye muscle she had
that I also had—I wouldn't go blind like she did, because I
got help. I didn't worry that those ladies, those girls, had
been anything that would make me something I didn't want
to be.

*I know, as much as I know my own name, that I would not be the me
I am without this land. And for most of my life, I believed this land was
poisoned. What on earth was I doing to myself. And for that matter, to my
children.*

"Can you be happy on this piece of land? That's the
only question I have. It's the only question you should

have." Mom sounded uncharacteristically clear. I don't mean that in a mean way. It's just that, even though she's practical, so much of her advice is clouded up in emotional language.

"Yes. I think I've found out that it's exactly where I can be happy. Where I had to come and be happy. I turned it around, you see? I went through the mirror, and now I'm out the other side."

"In the real world? Or the mirror world? Which one have you got now?" Now she was really sounding uncharacteristic.

"Well. God, I hope the real one. I hope it is, anyway." I was the girl in the picture, growing up here. I had a frame around me and I couldn't get out. But I got out. And I came back to close up that frame, break it up so it could never hold me again.

Was I saying all of those things out loud? Mom looked like she might cry, but then she busted out laughing. "Honey, I don't know what the hell you're talking about. I was just shittin' you. Look, you're sitting out here on thirty acres that backs up to federally protected forest. You don't have a care in the world. Get your damn goats or pigs or llamas or what the hell ever you want and get happy, dammit."

"Not pigs, mama. We got attacked by a pig."

"Don't be dramatic, Nicole. I've still got some fine barbecue in my freezer, thanks to your husband. Don't make a damn tragedy out of your happy ending."

CHAPTER TWENTY EIGHT

"So," CAROLINE STILL HAD the bunch of celery in her hand. She turned and pointed it at me and winked. "Your mama is coming. I had best tell you that Denise is coming, too."

I found myself staring deeply into Caroline's kitchen light fixture. I stared for a while. I was trying to decide whether it was a fixture I'd seen once in some fancy home decor catalog, a Mission-style copper number, or whether it was authentic. Caroline had a great eye for design. She might have picked it up in an antique store while traveling, or maybe—

"Honey," she snapped her fingers in front of my eyes. "Nicole. Stay with me."

"I'm sorry. To tell you the truth, I don't think it's gonna matter. I'm only trying to decide whether or not to text her and let her know."

"You don't think your mama will care? Cause I don't think Denise will care. We love her still, you know. Like we love your mama. We spent more than twenty years with both of 'em."

"You know, I don't. I know Mom won't care. Did I tell you, of all damn things, we ran into her Christmas shopping last year in Hudson Belk's? They stood there and hugged and cried, and then we all ended up shopping for knives..."

"*Knives?*" Caroline looked worried.

"No, steak knives. It was all okay, is my point."

Caroline went on, not completely convinced. "Well, I just thought I'd better tell you. So we could decide what to do. Charlotte said that since they were grown women, we should assume they would act like grown women on a family holiday occasion."

We both stood there for a second, but couldn't hold back a little laughter at the idea of what grown women may or may not do in this family.

"So Charlotte says, basically..." I waved my hand back and forth.

"Let the river run." Caroline held up her glass. I clinked mine with hers.

"Peace be with us all," I said. "On a related note, this wine is terrific. Is that a whole case over there?"

"Sure is. Denise brought seven or eight of 'em over when she left your daddy. I think she cleaned out his private stash."

"Brilliant foresight on her part. We might need more than one of those tonight."

Caroline drained her glass. "Donna," she began, "says there's still bad blood and they're gonna fight it out in the mud bog out yonder." She pointed out the window over the sink, toward the far end of her back yard.

"That could happen," I said, realizing I must have been considering the possibility, because I was eyeing that handsome light fixture again. "But then again, they've got so much in common."

I was more right than Charlotte or Donna, if you wanted to get detailed about it or you're keeping score. We all just kind of let them run into each other on the porch, late that afternoon. My mom said, "Oh look, hey, it's Denise! Oh, hey there, you! Come here!"

There was hugging, and some tears, and laughing as Mom spoke admiringly of Denise's boyfriend who had accompanied her to family Thanksgiving. "Brave AND Handsome!" she remarked. Once the wine got going, more tears and more tales from the crypt. You'd think any social event of any kind would explode after a statement like, "Honey, that day I walked in on you and that no-good husband of ours in my own bedroom, you did me the biggest favor of my life! It was like you gave me the keys to my jail cell!"

"If only I'd had the good fortune to walk in on him with that waitress—"

"*Which* waitress?"

"I *know*, right? Well, in this case, the one that served our rehearsal dinner."

"My *Lord from Goldsboro...*" blurted Aunt Lucinda, who was right next to me, hanging on every word like the rest of us and trying not to be obvious about it.

"So *that's* why she dumped that whole platter of Chicken Piccata on your lap!" Caroline interjected, filling Denise's glass. "*Now* it makes sense."

I remembered that night, sitting at the other end of the table across from my dad's best friend, Pete. Denise and dad had married during one of our brief speaking-terms intervals. After he'd been arrested for intentionally running over a bicyclist, but before he'd been kicked out of Little League coaching for hitting a ten-year-old boy with a baseball bat. That poor waitress—she dumped the platter onto Denise's eggshell white raw silk dinner suit, then ran off to the kitchen in a cloud of ragged sobs. All Pete and I had to do was look at each other. And that was accidental. We both knew what was going on.

"Two words: justifiable homicide." My mom's pronouncement resonated with the confidence of having said it many times. Denise nodded emphatically and wide-eyed.

Thomas walked past right behind me, having been dispatched to the garage for another case of wine. "Jerry Springer rule," he whispered. Thomas believes everything on Jerry Springer is real. I mean that those people are not actors, that those horrible stories, fights, grudges and trailer park operas are their real lives. He says if those weren't their real lives, then they all deserve Academy Awards and that we'd be wasting the best actors and actresses of our generation, of any generation, on after- noon TV while we were all watching movies full of stiff, rich pretty people. He's completely right, I think. The only difference between me and Thomas is that I didn't need to see it on the TV to know what a fucked-up life looks like, because I had a multi-channel view of the ways it can all go wrong.

We sat on the back porch at Donna's having our snacks. While everyone talked, I watched Nora and Edgar stalk and be stalked by Donna's enormous black swan. That bird and Nora had found one another on our first visit back out here, and they'd been in some mutual admiration cotillion ever since. Breathless and giddy, she and Edgar tumbled up the wooden stairs, Edgar clutching a single black feather.

"Harassing the waterfowl again?" I asked Nora.

"She is my spirit animal. And I don't mean in that creepy metaphorical sense everybody uses. She is an animal with whom I have transacted, and she now has temporary custody of my spirit."

"I hope y'all have some kind of paperwork to keep that straight." Maybe we could all use a swan-shaped caddy for our souls. It's dangerous to carry them around on your person sometimes.

"Creature of the night," said Edgar, smiling inscrutably.

"What else has your sister taught you?" I asked him, but he shushed me.

"Don't talk about Fight Club," he said.

"Nice."

"Hey," Nora protested, "I didn't teach him that. That was Thomas. Because he won't cough up any details about preschool."

Edgar shook his head. "Don't talk about—"

"I got it," I said. "Why talk about it? It's early yet. Just keep your eyes and ears open."

My brother Christopher showed up just before main course time at Caroline's. I saw his car coming down her driveway, so I met him where he parked, halfway to the house, next to the array of cars already scattered along Caroline's yard. Before he could even get his door open, I knocked on the driver's side window. He was talking to somebody on his cell phone.

"Gotta go. My sister's here. Yeah, my long-lost sister." He gave me a big smile, still listening to the person on the phone."

"Both our mothers are here. Right now. Inside. Up

there." I pointed toward the house. "Talking shit about our scumbag, no-good, lying sack of—"

"Jesus. Shit. Jesus. Somebody's gonna go all Hunter S. up there. I gotta go. JESUS."

"Oh, I'm knee-deep in fear and loathing already. And alone. But, to be fair, so far it's all good; they're both pretty liquored up. And they have a common enemy. And it's not either of us, so yay. But if you have another cigarette…"

Christopher shook loose a couple of cigarettes but he didn't get out of the driver's seat yet. I held onto the open door, mainly because I knew he wouldn't drive away if it meant dragging me down the road.

"Are there… firearms in that house?" I raised an eyebrow at him, because he grew up out here as good as I did, so this question couldn't be categorized as anything but rhetorical. "Jesus. Should I leave?"

"You're not really asking me that. And no, you can't leave unless you take me. And then we'll both be in trouble. Get out. Come on."

Arm in arm, we trudged through the gravel. They saw us coming on the porch and saluted us with various drunken expressions of affection for us, each other, and the world. I felt him stop and pull backwards.

"Don't even. Do not try to run. I swear I will make it so much harder on you if you run," I growled at him when I felt him recoil.

"You women in this family. You are all completely insane." Defeat, resignation, and awe. Yes, that's how to approach a family dinner.

"You forget. Neither of those women is related to the rest of this family."

"I'm not really talking about either one of them right now."

At the porch steps, I pushed him ahead of me. "Get in there, B team. I've been on since 2 p.m. Your turn."

Dinner was lazy and quiet, the music of forks and porcelain, cut glass and old soft wood under linen. Occasional low murmurs of appreciation, the words "who made" and "so tender" and "too much" and then "no more." Later at the table, over Caroline's grandmother's china, Charlotte was the first to deliver an impromptu speech of gratitude.

"I'm thankful for this very understanding husband of mine who brought me over all the way from Australia—ten thousand miles to spend this evening with my lovely ladies on the OCR, the old Camden Road."

I really had missed Charlotte. She could kind of be a bully sometimes, but I did always look up to her. She had more style than the rest of us, I guess. We hoped we'd pick it up in her wake, or at least enjoy it vicariously. She and I moved away around the same time, but she had kept going. Charlotte always had a softer place in her heart for animals than she did for people. To her, I'm sure they seemed a lot more reliable, supportive, loyal—all the things humans are supposed to be for each other, but for which our elders were not always particularly suited. Her mother was a beauty queen and her father was a pirate who looked like Hemingway. In my world order, Hemingway looks like Uncle Chuck. One way or another, Charlotte and Caroline spent a lot of time alone, just like I did.

Charlotte loved her dogs, her horses. She had this
big beautiful bay horse—I think it was a Quarter horse—I
remember I was so taken with him when I first saw him that
I ran up and threw my arms around his neck. She chastised
me. "One does not *hug a horse*." I apologized. To the horse,
not Charlotte. The whole thing confused me. But now she
had moved up from horses, having started an international
charity to preserve elephants—it was all very impressive.
It didn't surprise me, though. She always knew things we
didn't know and liked going *big*.

"Charlotte does love to exaggerate," Donna whispered
to Christopher, a little tipsy and giggly.

"No, Aunt Donna, I'm pretty sure it is at least ten
thousand miles to—"

Donna wasn't listening to me. She shouted over to
Charlotte, who was still in mid-pronouncement. "Honey,
we love you! We don't have any elephants here, but we sure
are glad you still come to see us."

Our elders. They continue to freak us out, and we
continue to confuse the hell out of them.

I was fiddling with my corn pudding while the speeches
went around the table. Christopher and I avoided eye
contact. Our mothers were sitting across from each
other, and we were uncertain what was going to transpire.
Josie was thankful for her sweet husband and for finding
Bertram, their big Irish wolfhound who'd gone missing
for a few days this week but showed up just that afternoon
while we were walking over to Donna's to start our evening
with baked brie, some crackers with a kind of hot jelly, and
pimiento cheese fritters. Josie had cried out with relief
when she saw him ducking under Grady Phillip's electric

fence, running through the sheep who were throwing a fit, hopping around and bleating like a devil wolf was after them. Bertram just kept shrugging his shaggy shoulders at them, slinking left and right, trying to avoid them while they ran every which way. Christopher was slinking that same way, sitting at the table, hunched and shaggy.

"Um, what's going to happen here?" He had leaned over as if to rub his right temple, but the gesture was a total ruse to keep his question private between the two of us.

"If it gets ugly," I whispered back, pretending to drop my napkin to lean closer. "I say we get out fast. No point in sacrificing ourselves. They're grownass women."

He nodded as he leaned back, seemingly comforted. Donna's former neighbor Jean was thankful for her grand-children, for friends, for wine. Good God I was thankful for wine. I wonder if I could just repeat that, or if I'd have to think of something else. Right now I was thankful I was last.

"... and all of y'all's stories, oh y'all just have *the* best stories. The ones about Little Granny feeding corn meal cakes to her doggies out the back door, the ones about Louella going to the mailbox in her panties—" Thank God for Jean. Yes, I could say that. Jean was our sympathetic audience.

"One day, Jean, she even forgot the *panties*. Oh God, that day I came home and came around that curve and there she was in the road, in one of Christopher's old T-shirts—mind you, he was eight years old at the time. And this was one of his old T-shirts—And I thought, what has happened here, and then she turned around—" Denise's eyes got big, and as she spoke, she waved her hands frantically. "Let me tell you, she turned around and it was a full moon. A skinny, leathery full moon."

Christopher and I both curled up in horror, letting out groans and disclaimers, begging to hear no more detail. My aunt Louella had been the family badass at one time, but her later years had been marred with... well, what more do you need than pantless trips to the mailbox. I don't know the source of the perception at the time, but I had always thought of her job as a telephone operator as glamorous and enviable. I still picture her as Veronica Lake answering a vintage switchboard. When in fact she worked for Southern Bell in central Florida in the seventies. Still, she sent me those pink-lined scallop shells wrapped in orange cellophane holding little silk orange blossoms and tiny bottles of orange perfume. I think I may for some time have had Florida confused with Hawaii. But Hawaii was where the Baptists sent Aunt Doreen. I don't know why Hawaii needed missionaries in 1972, but there you go. We got a shipment of macadamias from her. My aunts were always there to bless and to torment. For which part was I thankful?

I was thankful Edgar was so taken with his newly met cousin Gigi that he had not crawled under the table, and that he was sufficiently concerned enough still with maintaining Nora's goodwill that I could seat her next to him for a fairly worry-free dinner experience. I was thankful Nora long ago learned to eat a little meat at other people's houses, because if you're regularly eating fish and bacon, your vegetarian ethos is already questionable. I could see Nora was thankful she'd brought a pen so she could draw napkin portraits of wine-slapped grownups. I was really, really thankful for Thomas. There's people who tether you to this world who you didn't choose and who are not always helpful. For instance, I'll be a certified wreck if something ever happens to my mother. I won't know how to find my ass with both hands. I'll never be the same person again. But then there are people you find, as if you've been rolling around your whole life, dropped onto the floorboard of a fast moving car by somebody slamming on the brakes, and then one day you finally bump into the steering wheel again and drag yourself back upright. You don't let go of the wheel again, you just don't.

Thomas was sitting next to mom, picking at a salad of some kind with one of Caroline's grandmother's oyster forks. Once in awhile, he'd hold up a julienned bit of food item, gauge it, then either eat it or set it to the other side of his plate. He's not really a picky eater, but I had to admire his ability to find something else in the room on which to concentrate until the awkward spell was broken. I felt like it was close to adding up to something. And I knew he did, too, or we'd be moseying home, not dismantling a side dish.

Trying not to think about Aunt Louella's ladyparts and shiny behind lighting up Camden Road, I'd lost the thread of the table talk until I heard Donna's voice, a little shaky, and my name.

"...and I'm thankful, too, so, because you know Nicole, we just love y'all, we're so glad y'all are back where you belong, but I so wish you would not burn the house down. I know you and Christopher said y'all were gonna burn it down, but please don't. Because we love you. And we love Denise. She is family, too, just like your mama, and I just—stop it, Sam, I'm talking—" Donna was knee-walking at this point. But she could still spin a yarn without unraveling, so on she went: "I remember when I was twelve years old eating my birthday cake off these plates—Nicole, your daddy, we just can't do a thing about him anymore, but that house, Christopher you were born in that house—"

"Aunt Donna, I'm pretty sure I was born in a hospital."

"—in that house, and I remember that little record player you used to just play and play..."

I leaned over to Christopher. "Did you have a record player?"

"I don't know. She's drunk, though; it doesn't matter—"

"I think that was my record player—" I started, but Thomas and Christopher both just shook their heads at me slightly. Donna went on.

"Just don't burn down the house. All Denise's things she's got in there. And we love her, too, you know? It's okay though."

"Donna, I packed up my things a long time ago." We all shook our heads at Denise—she looked puzzled for a second, then held up a finger and nodded in understanding.

However drunkenly inadvertent it might have been, Donna did raise a relevant point for me. It hadn't ever occurred to me or to Christopher that his mother might have any attachment to the house, and for a minute I felt terrible about that indifference on my part. She'd lived there almost as long as my mother and I did. But as I watched her there with her boyfriend, the way she shied away from connection to it, I knew we hadn't been wrong. There was no one left to defend it. No one, it would seem, but Donna, and her dedication was kind of mystifying me. I couldn't even remember her having been inside it very often, despite having lived a quarter mile down the road. Maybe that was just it—the outside of it was a part of the OCR landscape. If you didn't have to go in it much, it was tolerable, even comforting, like relatives.

"...so my babies, please don't set fire to your old home-place." Donna beamed like a preacher backing away from the pulpit on a late Sunday.

I didn't have the heart to tell her the house was essentially condemned. Charlotte looked worn out. I knew she had wanted to see the house stay, too. For me, that house was the last of the line of poison that had kept us at a distance from each other all the way into our adult lives.

We were almost free. Why couldn't they let go of it?

CHAPTER TWENTY NINE

INEVITABILITY. IT'S A WORD I often ponder. I hadn't been able to get drunk enough to detach from reality by the time the speaking responsibilities fell to Christopher and to me. You never could be certain how Christopher might respond at an event like this one. He might just blurt out "I'm thankful I've got cigarettes and I'm next to last," or he might leave before he'd be asked to say anything. He's kind of the cat under the barn that way. He's grateful to be dragged out for food and affection, but you might get scratched up first. Edgar's turn had come before us and even he was thankful for *Star Wars,* so there was room to declare neutrality and be left alone.

When it was Christopher's turn, he went for old-school safety: he was thankful for his fearless cousins and his loyal mother. And for our still fairly new friendship.

"Man, this whole last year or so has been like one long fact-checking experience. Nobody put a rope around the tent to keep snakes out of it, you didn't cut the notches in the piano, those clothes in the attic aren't yours—Mom, did you know Nicole's not the one that drew those pictures on the Big Rock?"

"What pictures on the Big Rock?" Aunt Lucinda sat up in her chair. She might have been having a little doze, briefly. Everybody got quiet.

"Oh shit."

"What? What's happening?" Thomas and Nora both stared at me.

"What in the world? Pictures on the Big Rock. Well? Is

somebody going to tell me? Nicole, did you draw pictures on the Big Rock?" Lucinda could go from sassy Golden Girl to gingerbread house witch in a hot second.

"No ma'am. I absolutely did not." I may not remember everything from childhood, but I knew enough about my fear of the family monument the Big Rock that I didn't ever, ever deface it. I'm pretty sure I would have expected to be struck by lightning. In no kind of good way. For even thinking about it.

"Well, dammit. What's on it?" Now the whole table was under Lucinda's angry gaze.

Flustered declarations began to fly. Donna had not seen any drawings, but she hadn't been to the Rock in years, not since the Camdens' oldest bought the land next to it and built that big old house with the golf range, and now you had to watch for the golf balls, the dog was out and came back having half-eaten one, and then one came flying into the chicken coop and killed a little bantam. Beth had taken her kids over there, but she didn't notice any drawings, Josie thought she remembered seeing something when she had been over there looking for arrowheads, but the last time was years back, Charlotte and Dave were refilling their wine glasses, Nora was mouthing "what kind of drawings" to me, and I was shrugging while Christopher was waving "no" with both hands and laughing, and Caroline was already texting the Camdens to tell them we were going to be tromping through their backyard on Thanksgiving night so we could get to the Big Rock because everybody was arguing about it again.

The last big argument about the Big Rock had been between my father and my grandmother's youngest sister Ruth. Ruth became convinced my father had sliced off a piece of the Big Rock to ornament our then-new circular driveway. There was a big rock in the circle, but it was a no-name loser, nobody's monument. I don't know where it came from. Weirdly, it was missing from the driveway circle now. I don't even want to speculate what happened there. Mercifully, no one that I know cares. I may be the only person in the world who knows it's gone. And I don't care. So that's it.

"Lucinda, it's dark, and it got cold while we were in here eating."

"The temperature has dropped right much, mama." Josie patted Lucinda's hand and Lucinda drew it back like she'd grabbed a snake.

"Ruth came all the way from Bethlehem to make sure the Rock was still intact. I guess we can walk across the yard."

"*Bethlehem?*" Nora curled around my arm and held it tight.

"Pennsylvania," I cautioned. "Don't get dramatic."

"*What rough beast...*" My teenaged daughter quotes Stoppard and Yeats. I might have broken her. You have to be careful; kids repeat every damn thing you say.

"Besides, that's slouching *toward,* not *away from.*"

We were in a pack, some of us wrapped up in blankets, moving like a little human tumbleweed. I got tickled when I imagined us looking like the kids from a *Peanuts* special, bunched up and skittering across the Camdens' side lawn.

"Good God, all the trees are gone. I wouldn't a bit know how to find it now. Jesus, that house. It's giant."

"I forget what he does, he's got some kind of container business or something. Yeah, they cut down some of these woods for lumber before the Camdens bought this from—was it Justin? I can't remember whose it was. One of Gertrude's boys. Anyway, they have a very nice formal garden, but they left the Big Rock as a centerpiece."

I stopped walking and the crowd tumbled on.

"Wait. Wait. What?"

"It's okay—Caroline's got the code for the gate. We've been over there a whole lot."

Christopher piped up. "Branden and I didn't need any code. We just hopped the fence after they built it. We went to the Big Rock all the time when we were little. We played army men, space men—"

"Method Man & Redman?" I had told Christopher about the Waffle House encounter.

"That was much later, but yeah—"

"Well, let's not upset the Camdens on Thanksgiving—"

"Well, hang on a second, because I may be a little upset myself. At the risk of sounding like Aunt Ruth, if the thing is somebody's garden centerpiece, I think it might be ruined for me. The Big Rock ought to be a wild thing. Not a lawn decoration." I might have had some wine myself by then.

"That's a lot coming from somebody who drew peace signs on it." I couldn't even see which one it was in the dark, but everybody was laughing.

"Okay, if it's peace signs that are on it, then we know, do we not, that it was not me? Is there an anarchy A? Or a semicolon?"

"Or a Masonic eye?" Nora turned to Christopher. "Mom's in the Illuminati."

"I know." Christopher nodded.

"Oh, come on, Nicole. Nobody cares. What, you couldn't for once have done something wrong?"

I turned to look at Caroline. "Are you kidding? For once? Man, every single thing I did was wrong. Y'all always had each other—you, Charlotte, Josie and Meg. I had a book. You guys were all gorgeous, and I was fat and had glasses and braces. I was a damn disaster. I was just glad you all agreed to play with me, and I was never really sure why you would. And then you'd leave, and I'd be out here alone with them."

Now, after all the tears and hugging earlier, it would appear that I had brought back some additional level of emotional seriousness. Finally Donna stepped up.

"Nicky, we always loved you. But it was always so hard to see you." I knew what she meant, even though it probably sounded incomplete to some of the people out there on Thanksgiving night, next to the Camdens' fence, trying to decide whether or not we wanted to go look at a couple of sketchy boulders. "They didn't want us to see much of you, you know, back then. I guess we all know why now. We knew your daddy could be—well, awful in a lot of ways. But if we had known what you... and Christopher... Oh, baby doll. We would never have left y'all alone like that."

I tried to see Christopher's face, but it was too dark. I couldn't see anybody's face. We were huddled up like a bunch of druids or something, long blankets wrapped around some of us, black hulking figures with no faces.

"Oh God. Where's Edgar?"

I'd lost track of Edgar's little hand, and I started to panic immediately. Every inch of the nightmare rushed back to me, Edgar's face in the dream, his pale, cold hands the first time we came out here. The no-faced people in black.

"*Mom*, chill. He's right here. I told you I've got him." I'd never told Nora about the dream, the figures in black. I could see Edgar just barely, hanging on to her leg like a sidecar. She had a hand on the fence. They were ready to see what was over there. Fearless, both of them, in different ways and for different reasons. It was the wish I had made for both my children as I brought them into the world, because it's the only true freedom.

Fear. It's the smallest prison with the most people in it.

"Could that really be all it is?" I'm not sure I knew what I meant by that. But my family seemed to understand.

Donna—at least I think it was Donna—took my hand. "All anything is, honey, is what you think it is. Let's go, it's cold."

"I got to punch in this code to get in the gate here. I can't see squat. Somebody got a cell phone to put some light on this?" Caroline called out.

"I've got an actual flashlight." That was Thomas. He didn't go anywhere without a flashlight. Even if it was just the tiny Maglight he kept in his pocket with his cigarette lighter.

"Whoa, shit! Shit!!" Caroline shouted, and high-pitched screams cascaded through the cluster until we heard Christopher's voice calling out how that didn't turn out to be as funny as he'd hoped. He'd lost patience and jumped the fence while Caroline was punching in the code. In truth, I knew it just seemed more natural to him to get in the way he always had before. He could have had that code anytime, but he and Branden ran around the Camdens' yard like my high school friends and I used to run through the woods and the green of the sixteenth hole at North Ridge Golf Club, where my friend Lee's house was, setting off firecrackers and engineering water balloon battles. You can't transgress in the wilderness.

"I almost shot you, you little jackass. Just so you know."

"Caroline! Why do you have a gun, on your person, right this minute? On Thanksgiving?"

"You think people don't die on holidays? I'm sorry, Charlotte, but I'm a woman living alone down a dark country road. I have training. I have a permit. *On my person.*"

"And several cocktails. *In your person.*"

"Who said that? Christopher, you sassy thing."

"Well, you did almost shoot him just now—"

Christopher interjected, "Charlotte, that one was on me. If I were shot right now, I'd be cool with that. My bad."

"Do not," said Charlotte, "do *not* encourage her."

"I'm not a big fan either of guns myself, Charlotte, you know that. But if I were out here alone, I'd have one, too." I recognized Mom's voice and swatted at her to keep her out of this debate, but she was too far to reach, so I just windmilled to myself in the dark.

"Can we not talk about gun control right now? Y'all be quiet; I think the Camdens went to bed already." Josie tried to hush us, but she was just as loud.

"Not everybody celebrates Thanksgiving at Mardi Gras levels. They might be having a civilized after dinner coffee like normal people."

"You can't live on this road and be normal, Nicole. Thought you'd remember that much."

"I don't even think anyone is home. They're probably across the road at *their* homeplace. I still can't believe old Mr. Camden is gone." Lucinda's voice broke a little.

"Mama, he has been dead for twenty years."

"*That* long? Well, shit. I guess you're right. Marguerite is no spring chicken herself. Time, time, time. Why I can remember—"

"There it is." Caroline shined Thomas's flashlight up in the direction of Nora's voice.

Nora recognized the Big Rock from the picture I had, I guess. Or maybe it was the only giant boulder on its side in the vicinity; I supposed that's likely. She and Edgar trotted toward it, and so the rest of our little clutch skibbered over with them. I was laughing, not sure why. It felt like relief. I had been away from the land for twenty years, but it could have been as much as thirty since I'd seen the Big Rock. It was still big, and in this life, that's something.

"Charlotte, do you have a copy of that picture of our folks out here?" I'd seen the rock more in that photo than in real life. The photo held my aunts and uncles—and my dad—when they were all still children, not one of them yet a teenager. Before anything really bad happened.

"What picture?"

"What picture?" Donna echoed. It occurred to me at that moment that no one in that picture was there

that night with us. All dead or at a permanent remove. I
explained. No, I couldn't remember where I got it, and
no, I didn't know who took it.

"Is our mama in it?" Caroline asked.

"She is. She's in the middle. She has on this fabulous
1950s romper kind of thing. She's probably only twelve
or thirteen, but she already poses like a beauty queen. The
boys are all on the rocks around her. Uncle Danny on the
very top of the Big Rock, his legs hanging over the sides."

"I was probably not allowed to play with them that day,"
said Donna. "You know they used to run wild out in the
woods, all down in the creek. They'd come back soaking
wet, scratched up. Mama never knew what they were doing,
and she'd get so, so mad. I understand a little, now you
know, what with everything we know now about that boy
Little Granny and Grandaddy brought to live with them,
what the sisters all thought he was doing to the boys. But
back then, I just used to cry and cry because they'd leave me
at the house and run off, and I know now they would have
gotten in so much more trouble if they'd taken me, too."

I could hear the sadness coming into Donna's voice,
and I knew she was thinking about her sister. But then she
cackled. That's why I love Donna so much. All of them.
"One time," she said, and by this time we were laughing
too, because by the words themselves, "one time," we knew
the story was coming that would make it all feel better.

"One time Mama sat them down when they got back, all
covered in mud and blood and briars, she sat them down
and said, 'Lord help you children, the Devil lives in those
woods. Do you know that? And one day, because you won't
listen to me, the Devil is going to come and take you.' Well,

all the cousins, Danny, Nick and Bobby were giggling, and
Susan was acting like she didn't even hear, and Troy was
picking scabs off his legs—you know, they were not hearing
her a bit, and she knew it."

I shivered a little. The temperature continued to drop,
but we all just moved in closer to Donna. I knew the end of
this story, and I waited like I do for the one more chorus
of my favorite song on the radio. Everybody was chuckling
already. Somebody besides me must have heard it before.

"So the next day, you know, they did like always, went up
to Little Granny and she gave them a pail full of bread and
cheese, and they went out to the arbor and filled it the rest
of the way with scuppernong grapes and they went on down
into the woods to do whatever. I still don't even know what
all. Well, I don't know where she got one, ordered it from
a catalogue I guess or something, because I don't think
you could buy anything like this in Raleigh back then—or
maybe she made it, I don't know—well, while they were
down in the woods, Mama got dressed up in this costume,
all in red—red legs, red bodysuit, red toboggan with the
face cut out and horns on top. She must have used red
lipstick to red her face out."

The image of my Aunt Doreen, the Baptist emissary
to Hawaii, dressed up like the Dark Lord Satan has never
failed to cheer me. That cold night, it warmed my heart
even more.

"And she had an old pitchfork I reckon she'd painted
up. She grabbed that thing out of the cookhouse, and she
headed down Camden Road. Right down the center line.
Now I didn't see what happened—I don't remember much
of that afternoon until they were running back through the
front door and straight upstairs, white as ghosts, falling all

over each other and out of breath. Bobby's and Nick's faces were all red and tear-streaked—every one of 'em covered in mud. They didn't even come down for supper. I didn't know until I went up to bed what happened. Susan was up under the covers already. But she said they were playing, just like always, up in that field yonder. They had set up a whole pretend city that day, and they were arguing about which one of 'em was gonna be mayor, and they all wanted Susan except Bobby said a girl couldn't be mayor. And then they saw her, coming up the road. Only they didn't know it was her. Lord have mercy! They saw the Devil coming up the road to get 'em, and they all ran straight down into the ditch beside the road, covered themselves up with mud and leaves and waited for the Devil to pass them by. Then they ran home like their tails were on fire!"

As funny as this story had always been to me when my Granny told it, I was having trouble laughing along with everybody. I had been caught up by that wave of laughter, but then it turned, like when Edgar would have me read a line of a story over and over while he giggled himself to tears. Silly tears at first, but then the sad tears, that falling feeling. Lucinda somehow put her arm around me in the dark. I could smell the rosewater and feel the fringe of her woolly afghan. The emotion wasn't sadness. It didn't feel good enough to be vindication. But tonight, the image of my father in a ditch staring down the Devil was more resonant than it ever had been in childhood. Doreen didn't need a costume to be scary to me. I think it'd have been a toss for me as a kid, seeing Doreen or the Devil coming for me. But that bunch. That was a ditch full of pirates. They were all gone now.

"I don't know what these marks are you all have been talking about all night. Somebody's going to have to show me something. Thomas, where's that flashlight you had the foresight to bring with you? Thank the Lord somebody in this bunch has some sense."

"Right here, Lucinda."

"Now, which one of you knows how to find these things? Nicole?"

"Lucinda, I'm sorry. I don't have a clue what they're talking about."

Christopher stepped through the blanketed folks. "They're over on the side—here, Thomas, hand me the flashlight."

They were right. There were some markings on the rock, gray-black, worn. I'd never noticed them before, but they were so low on the rock some of them were partially covered by the ground.

"I really couldn't have made these. There would have been weeds and bushes—the Camdens have really cleaned this whole area out. We'd have never seen these growing up. I don't even know whether they were here or not back then."

"What are they?" Caroline's voice came from behind me. Nora shouldered up to the rock next to Christopher and crouched down.

"Well, Branden and I thought this one was a peace sign, but I don't think that's what it is now, looking at it..."

"Are they Egyptian? Hieroglyphics?" Lucinda suggested.

"No," said Nora.

"Nora would know. She taught herself hieroglyphics in third grade."

"That's your girl right there," Sam chuckled. "Nicole, I painted a lot of peace signs and that's not a peace sign; you're right."

Nora was trying to get a photo of the signs with her phone; little flashes lit our faces in short instances of recognition. "It's not working," she said "you can't see them with the flash, and it's too dark without."

"Well, has anybody ever seen any of these before?"

"Mom, you really *are* in the Illuminati—it's *you guys...*" Nora traced the strange circles and waves, her finger casting a shadow in the circle from the flashlight. "Oh wow. My *family* is the Illuminati!"

"We are definitely not the Illuminati," laughed Charlotte.

"Yeah," said Josie. "We'd eat the Illuminati for lunch. Especially if they wrote on our rock."

"You can tell the Illuminati to keep their hides off the OCR. We stick together. We don't need no secret handshake."

"Let me get up here and see this foolishness," Lucinda held onto Christopher's shoulder. "I can't bend like I used to, but just give me—well, good gravy, look at that."

"What is it, Lucinda? Do you know what they are?" Charlotte put her glasses on and knelt next to Lucinda.

Lucinda stood up straight. "None of y'all made those marks. I can't say that I know exactly what they are, but I have seen them before."

"Well, where'd you see 'em, Lucinda?" Donna asked.

"I can't be certain, but I'm pretty sure I've seen 'em in

Daddy's things. I'll check tomorrow. Come on y'all, before you catch something to die of out here in this field. Look at that pretty little fountain over there—Josie, they put that fountain in when they built this or is that new?"

"Mama, I think that's been here..." Josie took Lucinda's arm, and we all shifted as one, like a lumbering, shaggy beast getting up from a nap, to turn ourselves back to Lucinda's porch for dessert.

"Is it too late for coffee?" I asked

"Good God. It's never too late for coffee or prayer. Is there bourbon in the pecan pie?" Donna pulled her sweater tight around her waist. Caroline just laughed.

"Yes. Yes, lord. Is that a question? Have we met?"

I didn't need to look at Nora's photos to know that I'd seen at least one of those symbols before, and not that long ago.

CHAPTER THIRTY

I DIDN'T SLEEP AGAIN that night. All my plans for country living being the cure for my insomnia were turning out to be really problematic.

"Bad dream?" Thomas came out onto the giant porch attached to our tiny house. The sun was just coming up over the hill, the one across the road where the Big Rock still sat, still harboring the secrets of its markings like a mysterious new tattoo, souvenir of a drunken evening of bad judgment. Bad judgment, I thought. And I thought about how to say to Thomas that we can't live out here.

"No, actually. Not like they have been. Weird, for sure."

"I'll get the coffee pot and bring it out here. Hold on."

Thomas came out with the percolator I had bought recently. I guess I'm getting pretty fed up with artisanal shit. And anything that comes in packets or pods. I saw that percolator and I saw dinner parties with highballs and elaborate roasts with little socks on the parts that stick out. I do like perked coffee. I even bought sugar cubes for the sugar dish, but nobody here puts sugar in anything.

"Let me sit down. Seems like this one might be a sitting-down one."

"I dreamed I was riding a skateboard through this cluster of high rise apartments, shiny mirrored exteriors. I rolled past this neighborhood bar, people were saying hello. Then I realized I was on the skateboard because I was delivering Chinese food. I was in a kung fu uniform, and I had bags in each hand full of food. This really short woman came out of the bar and convinced me to deliver *her* to one of the apartment buildings, so somehow I picked her up, and we rolled along with the food to one of the big front doors.

"Inside, we got into an elevator, and I realized the floors were letters, not numbers, and I was relieved but I'm not entirely sure why—anyway, when we got out on her floor, most of it was destroyed. We were high up, no walls, just floor and some beams, some debris, plastic sheeting. But she kept saying, no, it's the right place, we just got some damage during 9/11."

"So what else happened?" Thomas went to refill my coffee, but it was still full.

"Besides me wearing a kung fu uniform and delivering Chinese food and a midget to a high-rise apartment building damaged in 9/11? Oh, nothing much."

Nobody said a word. It was cold, but I could still hear morning birds down in the woods.

I realized I was obsessing over a minute point. "Is 'midget' considered a negative term? I mean, is there a preferred..."

"Huh. Well. I don't know what the alternative would be."

"Yeah. 'Dwarf,' but isn't that something different?" It seemed really important to clarify all of a sudden, like I was failing at language and manners and life and everything.

"Yes—dwarfism is a condition where somebody's head is normal-sized, but his or her body is smaller. Midgets are proportional, just small. I think."

"Right. And with dwarfism, hands and feet can be relatively normal..."

"I think, yeah. But can we stop talking like we're Wikipedia?" Thomas smiled.

"But no other words for...?"

"Well, I've heard 'little people,' but that seems..."

"Oh yeah. Patronizing. Sure." Little people. I felt cold to the bone, but why?

Birds again. And the wind. Pretty far off, truck brakes.

"I'm really glad we got that straight," Thomas said.

"Yeah. Me, too," I said. Truck brakes. They were definitely truck brakes. But far, far away. Like a long, long beep. Droning.

"Can you see me?" Thomas put his face close to mine. I smiled, but he didn't. He looked at my forehead, petted it slightly, like he was taking my temperature.

"What are you doing, you freak," I laughed and shrugged, but I got my arms and coffee cup caught in my book bag strap. Why did I bring this book bag out here?

This is my book bag from high school.

Thomas. I was calling Thomas, but nothing was coming out. Everything behind him was bright white. There was a bad taste in my mouth, something choking...

Thomas's face was still and silent.

CHAPTER THIRTY ONE

THEN THE WHITE ROOM DISAPPEARED. I was standing halfway down the hill, past the house and the haunted garage, down near the floodplain. I couldn't see Thomas anywhere. But soon I could see Ben.

"You're a little confused. Oh, now, now." I was more than confused. Ben took my bag and gestured for me to sit down on the low stone wall that marked the east end of the property. "Doesn't look good. I know."

I sat down and tried to drink some of the coffee I still had in my cup, my cup I still had in my hand. It was cold and tasted bitter.

"Try again. You're a good girl, really. You require so little for consolation. Go ahead."

The next sip was hot. He was right. It didn't look good. If this whole thing were a movie, this whole turn of events would mean I was for sure, emphatically, big-time screwed.

"Jesus. How could I have been so stupid?"

"Not Jesus, my dear. No, no. Try again." Ben examined his ragged fingernails.

"Well. Am I dead?"

"Don't be *boring*."

"You found me in that parking lot on purpose."

"Guilty. Heh."

"You knew I wasn't having a fugue state."

"If I wanted a fugue state, I'd have brought one to you."

The porch, my little house, Thomas—everything was
gone. But I knew the low rise of the ridge and the dip of
the bottomland. I knew where we were. Shaggy Ben in his
big coat knew. He paced around, tamping down clods of
earth here, pushing mounds with the toe of his boot there.
He scanned the fields as if he owned... as if he...

"Oh," I said out loud, I think. I heard it. "Who are you,
then? Not 'Ben'."

"Well, you could say I'm a Has-Been..." He thrust his
hands deeply into his coat pockets and rolled back on his
heels.

"Okay. Fine. I'm leaving. How do I get back?"

"I am the Master here." Ben stood up straight and took
his hands out of his pockets. Did I see gloves? No. Had he
grown hair on his hands or had it been there?

"Where is here, then? Since I've always known something was wrong with it. Now I know who to blame. If I'm
in this much trouble, I may as well know why."

"This place." He started pacing again, down into the
crease of the fields, where the water moccasins roiled in the
summer. It was dry now, but the land did seem to undulate
with their narrow bodies as he got closer to it. I followed
him, even though I thought I wasn't moving. My feet
walked by themselves.

He turned to face me, walking backwards. "They opened
up the path and brought me here."

"Who?"

"You know. You know who was here. And not your
arrowhead makers. I've got no business with them. You saw
my return address, didn't you?"

I did. I couldn't tell anyone what I saw on the rock, especially when I saw no recognition in Thomas's eyes. He had taken a photo of Ben's mark on my palm. He knew the lines. But when he saw it on the rock, he said nothing. He had never seen it before. This problem goes back for weeks. Months. How long have I been here? Since Ben's arrival in my life? No. That's not right.

"It's not going to matter how long you've been here if you'll just let it go and listen to me." Ben held out his hand. It was getting really hairy, all up his arm. I tried to look in the folds of that big coat. "They called me, you know. The humans did. It's not my fault."

For a second, he sounded pitiful, and he wrinkled up his nose and pouted a bit. But it was a possum move. He was about to dive into me, and I needed to get in front of it.

"I know. I know how you got here. And she didn't bring you—she tried to send you back."

He grunted, a weird, pig-like grunt. "Who? You don't know anything," he whispered; he wasn't talking to me.

"That witch. She wasn't a witch at all. My father didn't know what he saw. She knew a spell or two, a good conjure woman. She could heal a wound or treat a summer cold with the plants she grew down there—" I pointed into the dark green of the very bottom of the land. "That was hers—" and I gestured up the hill to the shack in the woods. I was kind of making it up. Or I wasn't—I wasn't. She was telling me. For once, I was getting the message at the right time. I hoped it was the right time.

"My father said her hair was green. But it wasn't—that was the ash and the herbs. She tried to send you back where you came from. Nobody brought you here. You came here to hurt us."

Ben's shoulders spread and he grew bigger, it seemed, taller.

"Oh, you people brought me here. Why would I come otherwise? It's cold, and it smells like... plants. And disgusting, foul chemicals..." He writhed and snapped his head. "But no! I'm here now, and I can't go back without..."

Now he swept his arms around at something in the air and growled again. He acted like he was walking off a cramp, which might mean I was making progress, but at the same time I was pissing him off. Well, no way out but through.

"She didn't send you back. She cut you off, though. Until—" I thought about it for a second before I spoke, because I was about to take on something I didn't need, and for once I set the package at the foot of the person who ordered it. "This isn't my fault. I didn't let you back in here. He did. My father did this. And I don't have to pay for his mistake. You let me go back to my family. You don't have a claim to me."

"I have a claim to this land, and this land claims you! You came back here. You took it on. And this land is poisoned. Back to that cotton plantation. I came here with Sherman to burn it, and we *burned* it. I came back when that boy, that boy hobbled around out here, his mother praying for him to be healed, and I came and took him! They had to bury him in the woods because the Christians wouldn't let him in their precious land. But I came here first when the whip and the axe came down in this ravine. When the blood opened up the gate for me."

I looked at the ground under my feet, right where

Ben pointed. Blood bubbled up in the dirt, ropey like
water moccasins, deep red and thick, full of mud, my
feet sinking in it. We stood in the dark now, the hill
mounting up behind us. Fireflies were the only lights, and
they looped around my head with the cries of terror and
anguish. Human cries, but not human. *Don't let me see you,*
I thought, just like when I was a little girl in the house. In
the woods. *I know who you are but don't let me see—*

But I could see bodies. Bodies in the field. Bodies on
the ground. A foot, severed, beside a bloody anvil. A body
tied to the giant oak on the other side of the ravine, next
to my aunt's old house. The bodies were everywhere, like a
battlefield. But it wasn't a battlefield. It was a cotton field.
And the bottomland was full of the shacks, their lanterns
swinging in the night like the axes and the whips, and the
cries rang like bells.

I'd played in these woods. The stories I heard in them
were true. I had always known death was here, but I had to
prove it to myself. Not really. I proved it. It wouldn't have
come to this. What have I done?

I had lost track of Ben for some time by then, because
I was thinking about talking to Thomas, that day, months
back. Back in the real world when he took me out to the
Kron house on Morrow Mountain where I found those
girls' spirits. That day we realized my stories came from
some real place. On the way back to his parents' house, I
had been talking about this place where I was right now,
the bad land where I grew up. It was like the feeling that
kept me from following him down the hill to the family
Cemetery. I told him that I hadn't actually been afraid—
that woman's voice just kept saying 'There's nothing to see
there. That's not the place.' I mean, it was a little scary.

But it made sense—there was a child, I think, a child's funeral—some other stuff. It's a family cemetery, so it all made sense.

The land I grew up on is even darker, I had told him then, and I don't know why. I guess I always assumed something with the Native American history there. All those arrowheads. My mom thought she saw UFOs in those woods. It's that big—something *is* out there. But as far as I ever really knew, it had always been a big old farm.

"Big old farm?" Thomas had asked, raising an eyebrow.

All those years and I had never thought about it being plantation land. My great-grandparents had been poor. I guess in my mind I never considered the idea of what might have been happening before them. I remembered asking Thomas if we should research—maybe it *had* been. My ancestors surely never owned slaves or lived on a plantation.

Thomas had looked at me oddly, I thought, at the time. "Nic, I assume every square inch of the South has been touched by what you're talking about. Every square inch. Some things even Sherman couldn't burn away."

Ben was laughing, and it sounded like my father's laugh. I ducked involuntarily, but no one was hitting me. Blood was covering the ground all over, sticky and muddy. I must have fallen and braced myself, because it was all over my hands and arms, too. I felt sick, sea-sick, blinded by a pain in my head. When I stood up again, we were crammed, me and Ben, into the living area of our tiny house.

Chapter Thirty Two

CAR HEADLIGHTS HIT THE METAL of the stair rail and flashed for a second. Ben saw my face. That's why we were back here. I realized how he planned to do it now.

"Oh good—the family is here. Let's welcome them in."

His head, already shaggier and swollen, enlarged even more, and the curls of hair at his temples hardened into half-circles. He had to hunch over to fit under the low roof already, and as he grew longer even, he rolled his shoulders in a sinewy dance.

The door swung open. I tried to scream, but before I could, Edgar ran inside. Just like the dream, except this time I almost wished I'd see those figures a beat behind him. This time he was running toward the danger. He was running to me.

"Mommieeee," he started to yell, but he dropped to the ground suddenly, like he'd hit something. For a second, it seemed like Ben was surprised. But then he shouted at me in what sounded like a chorus of garbled voices.

"You can't protect them! It's over." He shook his head and snorted, pawed at the ground with his ragged Converse high top. Then he shifted a little, and laughed. "You're so boring. And stupid. You know, that's really it. It's exhausting how stupid you humans are. You must really be one, because you are seriously, fatally stupid. You don't get it yet."

No, I thought. But I saw Edgar stir a bit and begin to get up, so before Ben noticed him, I said, "I get *plenty*. You lied to me, and you broke the rules I made. I clearly said

'No manifestations,' and I meant it. You aren't invited here. And if I accidentally invoked some exception without knowing it, I hereby rescind your invitation. You're as bad as my father. You have *officially* pissed me off. Get out of my house!"

I reached into my collar and grabbed the St. Michael medal and closed my eyes. "St. Michael the Archangel, defend us in battle. Be our defense against the wickedness and snares of the Devil."

"Oh, now really. Stupid! Stupid!" Ben kept shouting over me, but I kept on.

"May God rebuke him, we humbly pray…" I could see Thomas through the crack as he tried to open the door, but it slammed shut before he could get inside. He pounded it with his shoulder, the thin wood buckling and bowing.

"Your superstitious crap. Criminy." Ben reached out his hand, hardened into something like a post, but then it curled and snapped. My pendant slipped off my neck and out of my hand, flying through the air until it split apart and scattered like mercury out of a broken thermometer. I didn't see any other avenues. And I knew if it wasn't doing something, he wouldn't care.

"…and do thou, O Prince of the heavenly hosts…" The door flew open, and Thomas ran to Edgar, picking him up and holding him gently by the shoulders.

"You idiot. You just won't quit. Let me explain something to you, since it's obviously too hard for you to understand, to analyze, to interpret the symbols. I thought if I made a little puzzle for you, since you like them so much. But no, it's taking too long for you to finish. You seem to have no sense of context whatsoever. So let me help you. Think about it. I just told you: the debt is open. Your father was never meant to be born. He died in a fire that never happened. The body that walked this earth had no soul, and the balance was broken."

Edgar was looking up at me. He could see me, but Thomas couldn't. He'd point, but Thomas would just turn his head back toward him, finger under his chin. I couldn't hear what they were saying, either because of Ben's yelling or the wind—was it coming through the door? No, it was coming from everywhere.

"...by the power of God, thrust into Hell Satan, and all the evil spirits, who prowl about the world seeking the ruin of souls."

"*Damn it all to Hell,*" Ben was shouting, waving his stick arms, "*why is it always those two lousy fucks who get all the name recognition?*" One of his horns got stuck in a wall while he was shaking his big dumb head around, and he had to shake it hard to get it out, a big chunk of tiny house coming with it. Thomas scooped up Edgar, covering his face and head, and stood up.

"What will you give me if I let them escape?"

"I'm not giving you anything, you Satanic bovine!"

Run, Thomas. I don't know if I'm right or not.

The name burned Ben like nothing else I had tried so far, and he recoiled, picking some insulation out of his fur and some fiberglass chunks off the ends of his horns. He seemed not to notice Thomas and Edgar as they disappeared toward the car. I had a few seconds.

"You look ridiculous." It was true. And I figured I

couldn't make it any worse for me. It got his attention.

"Honey, I can hardly wait until you get to see your true form. You think you've saved them. That's so... tired."

"Your display—that's what's tired. Is *Legend* your favorite movie or something? Me, I can't stand Tom Cruise."

"I don't have time for this. Dear: you can't save things that don't exist. Do you understand now?"

He was quieter. When I looked, the red in his eyes was gone. "Your father. It was a mistake. A *glitch*."

"There's no such thing," I said steadily, "as a glitch. Everything is either on purpose, or it's negligence."

"Well, then. *Mistakes were made.* Are you getting me? She owed us. Your Little Granny. Her boy should never have existed, which means you..."

He thought I wasn't following, but I was. I would not let him finish. I would not hear him. I put my hands over my ears.

"St. Michael. Be our defense!"

"Oh, shut up, really. You know what I'm telling you. You've known it all your life."

He kicked open the closet where Nora's photos were drying. Snatching them one at a time, he threw them in turn toward me. They flashed as they flew across the room; I threw my hands up to protect my face, but I caught one and looked. There were Nora's friends on Crybaby Lane, hugging each other in the dark. One lay at my feet of Thomas and Edgar on the swings at Pullen Park. I remembered that day, remembered buttoning Edgar's flannel shirt. But I wasn't in any of the pictures. One by one they

Ill-Mannered Ghosts

landed. Camping. Dinner at Caroline's house, their faces around the table. But not mine. And not Christopher's.

"There, there. Don't feel badly. It's not as if you don't exist. You're just a little less corporeal than you thought. Once, I thought I was brilliant painter. I forgot all about my assignment, I got so comfortable. It happens to us all."

Us all. An assignment. I didn't buy it. I don't think I bought it. Maybe I would have, if he had gone on much longer.

"Look, honey. You're nothing but a receiver. But it's not so bad, if you just accept it. Ha ha—get it? Because you're only a—oh, never mind. See, I can control all of it if you'll let me. You're sad right this second only because you've distracted yourself with an elaborate fantasy. Give me access again, and you'll forget all of it. You know I can fix it. I'm the sender. I control everything you receive. You think you've been here forty-nine years? What if you knew it had only been a few weeks?"

My head was hurting. *Just shut up,* I kept thinking, but I couldn't say it, and I wasn't even sure it was Ben anymore. I could hear my father's voice from him. Or I was imagining that part.

"He understood, your father. There are two kinds of people in the world—"

"Shut *up!*" I finally managed to shriek, "There are *infinitely* more than two kinds of people. I *hate* it when people say there are only two kinds of people—"

"That's right. Yes. Two kinds of people—the ones who can hate and those who can't. Your father knew how to ride that. You do, too. It can give you everything you want."

I tried to hold onto the idea that, considering my father's failed careers and dissociation from his entire family, this promise was a lie of great proportion. But everything was so damn noisy.

My head hurt like a splinter was forming from my scalp to my teeth. I didn't look at him, but what little I could see, Ben was taking himself back down to a less threatening size. His horns were soft again like blond curls.

"Yes, it's difficult. But you're almost there. I'm the sender—nothing you perceive comes from anywhere but me. But I need for you to be here, I need you to translate—well, me. I need you to bring me into this world."

Something was wrong, though. "Wait. That... doesn't make any sense. And what about Edgar? Edgar could see me just now. I mean, Thomas couldn't, but Edgar could."

Ben shivered. Just a little one, but I saw it when I finally drew up to look at him.

"I'm real. Edgar knows I am." One of Ben's eyeballs twitched, then it just kind of imploded. I don't know what else to call it—one minute it was twitching, then it was just gone, vitreous fluid running down his nose and cheek. He didn't react much, except to extend a disturbingly long tongue out to lick it away.

"You know what's real? What's real is that I could tell you," he smacked his lips, patted his cheek and the empty socket where his eyeball had been, "...is that I could tell you we were in Belgium, and you'd start eating these like *chocolate bonbons*..." Out of the empty socket, multiple eyeballs popped. Ben threw them at me in handfuls as they kept spouting out like a broken gumball machine.

"St. Michael! St. Michael—St. SOMEbody—I don't

know who I'm calling. Is anybody there? I don't know the RULES. Answer me! I'd like to register a complaint! Can I speak with Ben's superior? Not Ben... whatever its name is, because it's clearly not Ben. What is your name, you eyeball-flinging sack of shit?"

Well, that did something. He started to sway and unfold all over the place—what was left of the Ikea furniture started to splinter in all directions. Horns, scales, a long forked tail...

"Wow. What a cliché you turned out to be."

He was smoking and fuming when I saw her. I don't even know how she got in, but there wasn't really a door anymore. Or windows. Or a roof, really. So I guess she may have just manifested, or she could have flown, or, I don't know, burrowed through the floor. It had been a long day. I was kind of ready to believe anything.

But you might not be as ready, so you're just going to trust me, that I looked over and saw the Contessa di Castiglione perched on what was left of an Ikea chair. She stared over at Ben.

"I believe the lady asked for your name." That was all she said at first. Her arms folded across her chest, and she was swathed in a magnificent gypsy shawl or wrap or something with designs that appeared to move when you weren't looking directly. I mean, Stevie Nicks would have stabbed her for it. It was awesome. For a just a second, I forgot everything staring at the fringe.

"Come on. You know what you have to do." Her voice was electric but calm. Out from under that fringe, a pale hand, palm upwards. "Give it. You can delay, but you don't have a choice."

The garbled chorus shook the remaining kitchen shelves loose. Blue cereal bowls slid to the floor, rolling and shattering. "Marbas," they hissed, and spittle formed in the hairs around the mouth as it grew more and more snout-like.

"Can I ask *what* you are, Marbas, now that I know your name? Because you can't seem to choose a freaking SPECIES!" I grabbed one of my blue bowls as it rolled past. "I LOVED these bowls. I had to order them from Fab and I will NEVER find this color again." I let one fly toward his head.

"That's enough," the Contessa said. Ben—Marbas—the musk-ox pig-dragon—was vomiting all over my living room floor. "Sorry," she said, pointing at the area rug, "but the dry cleaner's not going to touch that."

"Well. It was cheap. And I wasn't that fond."

She furrowed her brow and arranged her wonderful shawl.

"Is this it? Is he leaving?"

The Contessa sighed. "You're the only one who knows."

I looked up at her and smiled shyly. "Michael?"

"Let's not get technical," she said, just before she laid a cool hand over my mouth. "I need to take care of a few things. Can you be quiet?"

"I think so. What things? Can I help? I'm real, right? He's bullshitting me about all of this, all the stuff about my family? Where are they? Are they okay?" Marbas had grown quite fat, and though he was having to drag himself along with brittle stick arms that kept cracking, he was actually still moving. The Contessa—I decided to call her Michael, anyway—she was watching him, but she put her hand back over my mouth.

"I'm seriously going to need you to stop talking. Let me see. Okay. That's odd. Well, okay..." She suddenly produced from under her cloak and handed me a clear box with a button. I almost blurted out my joy as I realized I was staring at the water ring toss game that was my favorite toy when I was about nine years old. It was no iPad, but it was at least as hypnotic. I got it for my birthday and I played with it day and night, pushing the button that forced air into the tiny water tank and tossed the rings into the air. The object was to hook the rings onto the pegs on the side of the tank. But the best part was just watching the multicolored rings just float down through the water. My cousins were visiting and they broke it. But here it was, perfect, and I pushed the button again and again until I heard Michael's voice.

"Marbas has something to say."

"*I'll see you in Hell,*" Marbas's voices hissed.

"Now, now. He means me, dear, and incidentally, there's no such thing as Hell." Michael slapped Marbas's fuzzy cheek, pretty hard, hard enough to shake his shaggy curls and knock some drywall off his horn. "Try it again."

"Sorry." It was the most disturbing apology I'd ever received, but it seemed sincere, and in this world, sincere apologies, disturbing or not, are rare. But I don't think I accepted it, and I don't think I have accepted it. It's not for me to accept his apology. And an apology will never be enough. He'll never be gone. I still see him sometimes. We brought him into this world, but we don't have the power to send him back. There's nowhere to send him. Hate can't be unmade. This fight never ends.

"St. Michael."

"I can't. It's a stain on all of you. It's not evil. It's sin. Two different things."

"Well, what do I do?"

"It's a disaster in here. What a small space—how can you work in it? I can't think." The Contessa crossed her arms.

Why has everything got to be so damn difficult?

"Lady, you've got to help me. You're all I have, and I am clueless how to proceed."

Ammonia... a strong whiff distracted me. For a second I thought the Contessa was about to help me disinfect the whole chaotic crime scene, but then there was a big blur, and I was lying on my back. A surgical mask came into view, and an arm reaching to something over my head.

"I'm trying to help you, honey. Slow down, though; I can't half understand what you're saying. Whew! You've been out for several hours; don't try to make it up all at once. Slow down and tell me what you need."

"Where is my family?"

The eyes over the surgical mask came into view as she bent down. I was in a hospital bed. The eyes had an awful lot of mascara on them, but they were kind eyes. They were kind, not sad, maybe smiling. It was an awful lot of mascara. Kind of messy. I reached up with a paper towel...

"Nobody ever thinks about how much crud there is to clean up after a demon vomits in your living room." That's what I was trying to say. And I was trying to clean up all the mess.

"Dear, do pay attention. That nice nurse is trying to help you. You know? Can't you hear her? You might want to talk to someone about this trouble you have with asking for help. Could you stop for a moment? My word. Why are you such a fretting mess?"

The Countess—Michael, whatever—was no help at all, except as ornament. Which isn't nothing, mind you. "You might consider your good fortune instead of complaining," she offered. I did not see her even reach for so much as a paper towel.

"Well, let's see. My tiny house is totaled. My family thinks I'm crazy. My father made a deal with Satan none of us knew for sure about, but whatever it was, nobody's likely to be surprised that he made one." I looked over. She shrugged one festooned shoulder, and her shawl fell down to her elbow.

So I kept going. "My entire family is cursed—"

"You do realize your terminology is all wrong. The 'curse' is lifted, and it wasn't even a curse, technically. And Marbas—Ben—is not a 'demon', though he is an asshole. English diction is so crude. Specificity is entirely impossible with you people. Your poets run around saying 'it is impossible to say, blah blah blah.' Goodness. Make a new language. Show some initiative. Excuse me; are those cigarettes?"

She wasn't wrong of course, but I don't like it when people pick on the way I talk.

"Our language works just fine for anything worth saying. It helps if you listen with some sense. You come in here like you know everything, but I don't think you pay much attention. Hand me that Swiffer stick, would you? I suppose *that's* one thing to be grateful for. I don't know what kinds of toxins are in this bile. I'm not touching it."

"Could I, ah, would it be okay if..."

"Sure, sure. Have a smoke. Take the whole pack. I suppose you can just puff away with impunity when you're immortal."

She shook out a cigarette and it lit as she placed it between her lips and closed her eyes. The room went back into shadow for a second. Then she looked over at me. "Oh yes. That's not bad. Parliament. That's an appropriate name for these items. They do facilitate conversation."

"Swiffer? The yellow stick behind you."

"Swiffer. I don't enjoy saying this word."

"Me neither. But I enjoy having a stick that cleans up dog fur and demon vomit."

I cleaned and she smoked. Two trash bags full of wrecked Ikea furniture, broken dishes, disgusting towels, some fleshy bits I tried not to think about too hard. Glass. Some fur that I hoped had been part of his clothing.

Finally I decided I just couldn't hem it all up. The more I cleaned, the more dross there seemed to be. In the corners. All over the little stairs. The ceiling, for fuck's sake. It was hopeless. I slumped down on the charred sofa. Michael walked over and handed me one of the cigarettes. She brought my broken blue cereal bowl she had been using as an ashtray and set it between us. "Don't take it so hard. It's almost over."

"That's what I'm afraid of."

"You people. It's always almost over, and you just don't know it. It's just a little pinprick. Over in a second."

"And nearly painless. I've heard this before"

"Nearly painless. I suppose. Let's say so."

We sat quietly for a little while longer before she stood up and arranged her shawl. She looked at the near-empty pack of Parliaments, held them to her cheek for a second, then dropped them to the ground.

"You know there's only one way to clean this up," she said.

"A fire." I answered her, no more thought necessary.

"Yes, girl. But first—" she fussed again with her shawl, "why not take a photo of me?"

I was cheered irrationally at the prospect of photographing the Countess, or at least the feeling of photographing Michael as the Countess, and for a second, anything seemed not only possible, but likely. I looked around for one of the cameras, but the devastation had rocked everything out of its place.

"Here," she said, picking it up off the remains of the table, "just use your phone."

And then I couldn't see. I do hate a flash. I thought I had the damn thing turned off.

CHAPTER THIRTY THREE

"HONEY, LET'S TRY AGAIN. I can see those eyelids a-flickering. I know you're in there. Can you hear me? Let me let you see—" The nurse moved aside, and there they were. White room, all of them, Thomas sitting on the side of the bed. Nora half asleep in an orange chair with Edgar in her lap. I started to cry, because that's what you do. "They're all right here. That's right. They've been here the whooooole time," my masked friend said, consoling.

"What happened?" I mean, what else am I going to say.

Thomas patted my foot. "Hey, baby. Welcome back."

Nora set Edgar on his feet and came over to the other side. The nurse ducked out the door, waving her hand dismissively at us all. She's awfully cavalier about this, I thought. I must be okay.

"You checked out." Nora said. "Please do not repeat this activity."

"We can't live on that land," I said firmly.

"What? Are you still talking about the farm? I thought we had that figured out weeks ago, baby."

"Where are we living? Are we living in a tiny house behind where I grew up?"

"With a bunch of tiny men making tiny shoes?" Nora laughed, so I laughed. Oh boy.

"We didn't sell our house and move out to the land to build... I guess we didn't."

"We did talk about that. But when we went out there

to visit, we stood in the yard of your old house and you turned around and told us all to go to Hell, basically."

I hoped those hadn't been my actual words, because it felt like I'd just had a glimpse of a return address. A timeline was getting easier to see. It might take a few days.

"My phone—"

"I already called your mother and she'll be here—"

"Just get me the phone—"

I pulled up my photos. There it was. Against all explanation. A broken blue bowl, two cigarettes resting. Even more against explanation: my unmitigated relief.

"Nic? Did you find what you needed?"

"Yeah. I did, I think." My family stood around me, all around the edges of the bed. I'd go home tomorrow. To my real home. I had a lot to think about. But not tonight. I fell asleep, finally. It felt like it had been weeks.

When I woke up later, they were all there. Thomas was by the door, leaning on the frame, talking to a woman in a lab coat with a stethoscope poking out of the pocket. I watched them. He was nodding, but kind of smiling. I could only hear a little.

He saw me watching and smiled bigger. When he took my hand, I said, "I heard what she said, but I'm not scared now."

"What?" Thomas looked very serious then. "What... do you mean exactly?"

"I heard her say it. That they often try again. But I know his real name now and he can't get me. That's how it works. Don't worry. I've got this."

*I know it probably sounds crazy. Don't worry. I know what I've got to
look out for now. You might not think I do, but really I do. It's just the words
for it are so imprecise and ugly.*

"Whatcha want to do?" Nora asked, smiling.

Some things you don't have to decide. "I want y'all
to find an NCIS marathon or something, because CNN
is getting on my nerves. Edgar, bring me that coloring
book and hop up here. Is this rice pudding over here?
Who wants to share it with me? Because if I eat this whole
container, I'll be ill."

I love the smell of pencils and rice pudding. My family
close up, the sounds they make settling down to rest after
work. I love these things. Everybody has them, the places
you will always inhabit, even once your body leaves this
world. These are the places I will always be.

She's there most times. When I check the photos on
my phone. Sometimes it's Justine, though, her smirk and
cocked hip, her painted nails around the cigarette, smoke
in her hair. Sometimes it's a lady with little explosions
beside her head. Sometimes it's just a cigarette perched in
the crack of the blue bowl. Sometimes it's two cigarettes,
burning away to ash.

I don't know what it means, but it's proof. I was there
and she was there. Did she come here or did I go over? It is
impossible to say. But it's as likely as anything. It's something to hold onto like a handle until more research can be
done.

Epilogue

I COULD HAVE HALLUCINATED most of this. Either way, after what had happened, he can't come back.

But three days later, just in case, I snuck out to the Big Rock and chiseled off every damned mark I could see.

About the Author

Nicole Sarrocco, the author of this *Occasionally True* series of novels, lives in Raleigh, North Carolina with her husband and two children. Raised on a tobacco farm on the Wake-Johnston County line, she has a PhD in English, and loves teaching high school. She never has pretended to be normal, but does claim that good manners are in her regional DNA.

CPSIA information can be obtained
at www.ICGtesting.com
Printed in the USA
FSOW01n2324140316
18000FS